Peppermints & Pandemonium

Marcall's Breakfast Cafe Paranormal Cozy Mystery

B I Skinner

Contents

Chapter One

"Aaaaiiiieeeee!" The scream echoes throughout the Hotel Glacier ballroom during the Crested Peaks Christmas Party.

"Don't tell me there's another body!" I hear someone say as everyone in the ballroom quickly looks around to see who died this time.

Detective Andrew Bailey, who is also my boyfriend, glares at me as if to say, don't even think about it.

I hold my hands up in mock surrender. Even if we have another murder in our picturesque mountain town, I'm done with playing the investigator. I have a successful vegetarian breakfast café, that I inherited from my beloved grandmother last year, which keeps me plenty busy.

And I have sworn off any future crime investigations. I don't care how many bodies there are. And for such a small town, we seem to get a lot of murders here.

Drew sighs. "I better check it out. But you stay put," he tells me.

"Keep an eye on her, would you?" he adds to Damien, who is always the more cautious one in our group. He's also the chef at my cafe, Marcall's. He's even more cautious lately since he and his husband Tom took in a three-year-old foster daughter.

"Got it, detective." Damien nods his head in agreement.

"I'm not a child, you know!" I protest.

Meanwhile, Damien and Drew kind of shake their heads like they think that's debatable.

Can I help it if I have connections and skills that the Crested Peaks Police Department doesn't have? And what is a girl supposed to do when her way of life, and the town she loves dearly is threatened? Do they seriously expect me to sit back and let bad things happen?

"Do you think there's another body?" Miranda, my best friend and witching mentor, asks, suddenly appearing at my side.

"I'm just glad I didn't find it again - if there is one, I mean," I respond with a shrug rolling over my shoulders.

"Or that one of your familiars found it," Miranda points out.

Besides Marcall's Breakfast Cafe, I inherited my Gran's familiars, Marshall and Marcus, who she named the cafe after. They're a pair of talking rabbits who have this uncanny knack for discovering dead bodies.

Their sidekick, Stumpy, is a cat who has stumps for back legs. They invited him to live with us one day without telling me. He doesn't talk to me, but he tells them, and they translate. Even he found a mobster's body in the park last spring.

Drew returns after several minutes with a relieved look on his face. "It was a poltergeist in the ladies' bathroom," he explains.

Miranda, Damien, and I all breathe a sigh of relief.

"How crazy is it that we all jump to the conclusion that there's been another murder here, huh?" Miles, Miranda's boyfriend, asks.

Rumor has it that there's a betting pool circulating through Crested Peaks on whose body I'll find next. I still haven't figured out who's running it if it's true, but I hope those days are long behind me.

"Hey Charlotte, we didn't get a chance to thank you yet for the unicorn cupcakes you had delivered to the house," Tom, Damien's husband, tells me.

"Was Poppy excited?"

"She was over the top excited," he says, nodding his head. "Although when I say over the top, I mean she doesn't want to eat them because they're so pretty."

I put my hand over my mouth to keep from laughing. "I never realized that would be a problem!" I exclaim.

"Three-year-olds are weird," Damien informs me.

Our friend Chloe, who is a witch-like Miranda and me, runs Chloe's Cupcake Truck, and she makes these incredible cupcakes with enchanted decorations. Because Poppy is obsessed with unicorns, I thought she would enjoy some. I didn't realize she might take them a little too seriously.

"I'm glad she's enjoying the cupcakes, at least. Even if she refuses to eat them."

"Yes, but what happens when the cupcakes go bad?" Damien asks.

"Tell her the unicorns ran away?" I suggest.

"That won't give her nightmares or anything," Damien says.

"Tell her Bubbles ate them instead?"

"You're not helping," he informs me. "Then she'll think the dog has unicorns in her stomach."

This whole raising children thing is a lot more complicated than I realized. Poppy and her mother came here from Puerto Rico but then her mother died, leaving Poppy in the hands of the Department of Health & Human Services.

They've been searching for months for Poppy's relatives with no luck. If they can't find anyone, Damien and Tom plan to adopt her permanently.

"Greetings, friends!" Harvey calls out as he flies over our heads.

"Hi, Harvey! Merry Christmas!" we call out to our friend, the ghost. Yes, it's a little weird to have a ghost for a friend, but it is Crested Peaks where paranormals of all types live together.

Harvey is a ghost who lives at the Hotel Glacier. He was killed in a shootout in the late 1800s that occurred between a bank robber and the sheriff. He's invaluable in gathering clues and gossip when we need it. No one thinks to watch what they say or do in front of a ghost. They're practically invisible, after all.

"Can you believe that poltergeist?" he asks, shaking his head sadly. "As you all know, I try to keep a handle on things around here. I know that folks come here specifically for the paranormal experience, but there's no need to scare them unnecessarily. Especially when one is using the indoor facilities."

"Did you set him straight, Harvey?"

"I did. And he's banished for the evening. I told him he could just think about what he did while everyone else gets to enjoy the party." He then folds his arms across his luminescent chest in a self-satisfied harrumph.

"Oh, dear!" he exclaims as he notices another problem cropping up across the ballroom. "My job is never done," he grumbles, zooming off to deal with what appears to be another poltergeist, now throwing appetizers into the fountain in the lobby.

"Looks like the poltergeists have been drinking the spiked punch tonight," Drew laughs. I can tell he's extra relieved he doesn't have to investigate another murder now.

During the Halloween party this year, the town's mortician dropped dead of what we all assumed was a heart attack. Except it turned out to be a murder. I'm sure Drew would like to enjoy a party for once without having to throw work into the mix.

"They went all out on the decorations this year, didn't they?" Miles points out as we all look up at the enchanted ceiling. The Hotel Glacier was built shortly after the heyday of the Colorado Gold Rush. They spared no expense in creating the opulent building, which was one of the first to have gas lighting indoors.

They hauled bricks and tile over treacherous mountain passes, and much of the same architecture and designs remain. Tourists come from all over to stay here, both to admire the century-old designs and hoping to spot one of the many ghosts who live here.

Although I doubt they appreciate being startled by a ghost in the bathroom or pelted with appetizers while trying to take pictures in front of the picturesque lobby fountain.

This evening's magical Christmas decorations feature a starry sky with an authentic-looking shooting star now and then. There's also a magical Santa and his reindeer that fly across the ceiling once an hour while Santa shouts, "Ho! Ho! Ho! Merry Christmas!"

It's a formal event with everyone dressed in their best holiday fare. Lots of ladies in sequins and men in tuxes. Not surprisingly, Drew looks extra fetching in his tux.

Gladys, a regular in the cafe and fan of my boyfriend, has stopped to visit with us several times tonight to flirt with Drew. I should point out that she's old enough to be his grandmother, but she enjoys batting her eyes at him.

She often laments that as a detective, he no longer wears a uniform which she prefers to see on him. So, it's no surprise that she's admiring him in his tuxedo this evening. "Why, if you don't look like you could be the next James Bond Detective Bailey."

"Oh, Gladys, you're always good for my ego," he tells her.

Meanwhile, I catch Damien and Tom nodding their heads in agreement. They like to tease me about how handsome he is by calling him Detective McHotty behind his back. I get it. He's tall and athletic, and his emerald green eyes are stunning.

But I wish he wouldn't get so frustrated when I try to help him investigate the numerous murders that have happened since I moved back to Crested Peaks. But that's okay because I've sworn off any future private investigator work.

I knew Andrew or Drew, as I call him now, in high school. He was my first kiss. And then he ghosted me for ten years. And not the good kind of ghost like Harvey. He stopped speaking to me. Naturally, as a teenager, I assumed it meant I was a horrible kisser, and I was mortified.

But the truth was his parents forbade him from talking to me, and his friends told him he shouldn't go anywhere near me. My mom was a witch, and my dad was a wizard, but more importantly, they were crooks.

Con-artists, to be precise. And everybody knew it. That's why Drew's parents didn't want him anywhere near me. It's also why I swore off my own witchcraft skills for nearly a decade.

My parents were killed in a con job gone wrong when I was young, and I moved in with my grandma. The second I graduated from high school, I split for New York.

I wanted to put Crested Peaks and everyone who knew about my parents and me as far behind me as possible. In Manhattan, no one knew I was a witch or that my parents were criminals.

Ten years later, Gran died and left me everything. To make matters worse, my fiancé dumped me to appear on a reality tv dating show, and when I mixed up my boss's girlfriend with his wife, I got fired. It seemed like the perfect time to get things straightened out in Crested Peaks. I didn't have anywhere else to go after all.

I never intended to stay in Crested Peaks. I planned to sell the cafe and my grandma's house and figured I'd take her rabbits with me wherever I went. But I didn't realize that my grandma's ability to talk to the rabbits must have transferred to me when she died.

Imagine my shock when I opened the door to Gran's house, to find her pair of saucy rabbits demanding parsley. I thought I was hearing things at first. Or I'd finally lost my mind.

My grandma always claimed she won them in a poker game, but that was decades ago. Do you know anything about rabbits? One thing I can tell you is they don't live for decades, so I've always assumed they're enchanted. Aside from the talking thing.

They've even made very good junior investigators when I need help solving mysteries. They overhear conversations and have connections all over town with the other animals.

There was also the small matter of me pretending I wasn't a witch for most of my life. My skills were rusty, to say the least. However, Miranda has helped me regain some confidence and magic skills.

Damien was the chef at Marcall's when Gran was alive and thankfully agreed to stay on when I took over. I don't know what I'd do without him. He was a young Cuban emigrant when his family moved here, and many of the recipes he has developed for the cafe are inspired by his own grandma.

He even invented the Damien Special, a breakfast burrito with eggs, beans, cheese, potatoes, grilled jalapenos, and caramelized onions, along with a secret sauce even I don't know about. We have tourists who show up from all over requesting it. It's particularly popular among the skiers before they hit the mountain for the day.

My plans to sell everything and leave Crested Peaks grew into the dream of fulfilling my grandma's legacy of running a successful café. Then my friends became the family I never had.

And here I am, over a year later, drooling over the decadent dessert bar with Miranda – just one more time – we both insist. But we know it's probably a lie. The mammoth display is in the middle of the ballroom and spans numerous levels that reach at least six feet high.

I tease Miranda because she can't reach all the way to the top. At 5 feet 10 inches tall, I tower over both Miranda and Damien. And tonight, in heels, I'm taller than almost anyone in here. Except Drew.

I compliment Miranda on tonight's hairdo, which she often changes by the day. Tonight, she's wearing it down to her waist in cascading mermaid colors. Tomorrow it might be short and spiky and bright green. One of the many perks of being a witch.

Miranda and I have the most fun changing hairstyles and colors on a whim. I'm wearing mine red tonight with what appear to be tiny sparkling white lights but are just an illusion. Who puts lights in their hair, after all?

It's almost impossible to choose just one dessert from the display. Each level rotates slowly as the exquisite delicacies move by. But I nearly drop the sparkling red and green dark chocolate truffle I've just picked up when another woman's scream splits the festive air.

"Aaaaaiiiieeeee!" echoes across the ballroom, only this time it isn't coming from the bathroom. It's coming from a woman who's staring out of the floor-to-ceiling plate glass windows on the opposite side of the room. Every head in the room swivels her way, hoping it's nothing but another ghostly prank. "Santa's dead!" she shrieks.

Chapter Two

Miranda and I stare at each other wide-eyed.

"Please tell me that's part of the show," she whispers. Earlier in the evening, they treated us to a spectacular water fountain show for which they used magic to purposely melt the water in the lake.

But the woman continues to scream and point as several other party revelers rush to the window to see about all the fuss.

"Oh, no!" cries one of the men pressing his face up against the window to see better. "Someone call 911!" he turns to the crowd and shouts. "Santa drowned!"

I scan the room looking for Drew, and he's already on the phone while striding toward the window. This can't be happening. Santa can't drown right before Christmas.

The only person I know dressed as Santa tonight is Jack Frost, the owner of Santa's Workshop Toy Store on Main Street. I bought Poppy a stuffed unicorn there last month. It can't be him. It just can't be.

I hope it isn't anybody. Please let it be a fake Santa. Someone's house decoration that blew into the lake tonight. Even though it's been calm all day, maybe the wind picked up tonight while we were all in here, and we didn't know it. Or perhaps some kids stole a decoration and threw it in the freshly melted lake as a joke.

Drew strides quickly past us, and as I stare at him with my hands up to show we'd like to know what's going on, he holds up a finger to say, hold on while he keeps walking toward the stairwell that leads to the entrance facing the lake. Miranda sighs loudly beside me. "This can't be good," she whispers.

Murmurs and whispers fly around us. I hear some talking about how they saw Santa drunk tonight. Still, others talk of how he's drunk a lot. A small group of women next to us complain about how there's too much alcohol available at these parties, while another complains that there's too much alcohol available in Crested Peaks period.

Miranda gives them her best salty look. "We don't even know if there's a real person in the lake, and they're already armchair quarterbacking about too much liquor in Crested Peaks," she complains loudly enough that several of them turn to shoot a dirty look back at her. The familiar sounds of sirens split the frosty night air, and I know then Santa is no fake.

"Do you think we should go down there?" I ask as Damien wordlessly appears at our side. I swear being a dad has given him radar when it comes to even a hint of someone getting in trouble.

"You both know Drew would tell you to stay here and let the professionals handle it," he scolds.

"We could stand on the sidelines and watch, you know. It's not like we'll be in the way." I propose.

"I agree," Miranda says. "I want to know what's going on. If that truly is Santa, how did he end up in the lake?"

"He got drunk as usual and stumbled out into the cold and drowned. It's obvious if you ask me," one of the arrogant busybodies near us offers.

"No one asked you," Miranda sneers at her with a huge fake grin on her face.

"That's our cue to leave," I insist, grabbing Miranda's arm steering her away from the group of pretentious ladies. That's all we need now is a brawl in the middle of the ballroom, while who knows what is happening downstairs.

"Don't say I didn't warn you!" Damien calls after us as we hurry the same way Drew went.

"This will look so bad if there's another death at a Hotel Glacier party." I point out.

"Less than two months after the last one, too," Miranda reminds me.

"And we already had enough terrible publicity when the soap opera star was murdered here last month!"

Miranda and I watch the commotion from the shadows as crews from the ambulance try fruitlessly to revive the victim they've retrieved from the lake. We can see the Santa costume, but we still don't know for sure who it is.

But when they place the man on the gurney for transport, we see his face, and it's definitely Jack Frost. Several of the partygoers who joined us to watch gasp out loud when they realize who it is.

The paramedic works tirelessly, pushing on Santa's chest while they load him into the back of the ambulance. It doesn't look good from this angle. The uniformed police officers who are on the scene slam the doors shut allowing the ambulance to speed away. They both huddle with Drew, all three of them shaking their heads, and it appears that Jack Frost is toast.

"That's so sad," one woman says behind us.

"I bet he got drunk and fell into the lake by accident," another woman speculates. This time Miranda says nothing because it looks like the woman is right.

"At least it wasn't murder?" I offer.

Miranda shakes her head. "You had to say that out loud, didn't you?"

"What?" I ask. "It looks like he fell into the lake and drowned. How much simpler can you get than that?"

Before Miranda can answer, several other police officers show up and Drew marches back to the building before Miranda and I can hide. Uh oh. I know that look, and he's in a bad mood. And just as I'm hoping he doesn't notice us, he stops.

"Of course, you two had to be right in the middle of this," he grumbles.

"To be fair, we really aren't in the middle of anything. We're watching from the sidelines, and we aren't in anyone's way," I point out.

Drew sighs heavily. "You're right. I apologize. It's a shame, that's all. It looks like he had too much to drink, wandered out into the cold, and then fell into the lake. Poor guy probably didn't even know what hit him."

"You don't think the paramedics can revive him?" I ask.

"They aren't sure how long he was in there. If the water hadn't been melted for the show, he probably would have just passed out on the ice where someone might have seen him. But this way, he was submerged for a while."

Once there's nothing new to see, the crowd disperses.

"We sure know how to end a party around here, don't we?" Miranda asks.

She's not wrong. First, it was the 4th of July stabbing at the town festival, then the poison cupcake at the Halloween party, and now we have a drunk and drowned Santa at the Christmas party.

When Drew's phone rings, he excuses himself, saying it's from the hospital.

Miranda and I head back upstairs to fill in Damien, Tom, and Miles. Everyone who's left gathers in small groups, whispering about what could have happened.

"The stories are flying fast and furious. Please tell me you know what happened," Damien begs.

"Oh sure," Miranda teases. "When we sneak off so we can find out what's happening, you're full of warnings. But when we get information, you want to know all about it."

"Yeahhhhhh," Damien responds, still waiting for us to fill him in.

"It appears he got drunk, wandered out the back door, and accidentally drowned in the lake. Drew said they don't know how long he was submerged in the water."

"But they took him away in the ambulance?" Tom points out.

"They were doing CPR on him when they left, but I'm not hopeful. The hospital called Drew, so we came up here. He should have more news soon." I tell everyone.

"Here comes Drew now," Miles says.

Drew joins the group, shaking his head sadly. "He didn't make it," he whispers, hoping he won't draw any more attention than we already have.

"Do they know if he was drunk? Is that what killed him?" Miranda asks.

"The autopsy is scheduled for tomorrow, so we'll know more for sure then."

Despite his efforts to keep things on the down-low, we're approached by the same group of women who were gossiping before about how there's too much alcohol in Crested Peaks.

"Detective Bailey," the first one says in a voice that reminds me of that lady from the Wizard of Oz who tried to take Toto away from Dorothy. She looks like her too.

"Mrs. Schmidt." Drew nods his head at her and the entourage following her.

"Can you tell us what happened to Mr. Frost?" she asks.

"Sadly, Mr. Frost passed away on the way to the hospital."

She eyes all of us with distaste. "We already assumed that. What we need to know is did he drown because he got drunk while overindulging on the free-flowing booze that seems to be everywhere this evening?" When she eyes the bright red cocktail that Tom holds in his hand, he blushes and looks at the ground.

"We should know more tomorrow when the autopsy is complete," Drew patiently explains. From the pinched look on his face, I gather he's interacted with this woman and her group before.

"I would think as a man of law enforcement you would be opposed to the abundance of alcohol at events like this."

"As long as no one is driving while intoxicated or serving minors, Mrs. Schmidt, that's all I'm interested in," Drew responds.

She glares at our group once again, makes a strange tsking sound, and stomps off, her crew in tow.

"What was that all about?" I press Drew.

"She runs a group called the Women's Anti-Liquor Coalition, and if they had their way, they'd eliminate alcohol entirely from Crested Peaks."

Miles gasps as if he couldn't bear the thought. He's a craft beer aficionado, and still laments that the tavern next door to Marcall's turned out to be a front for organized crime.

Miranda snorts. "Like that would ever happen!"

"I don't know," Drew says, "they're always pressuring the city council to enact stricter regulations in town regarding alcohol. Remember last summer's ban on hard alcohol in restaurants after 11 PM?

"I do!"

"That came about thanks to that group," Drew informs us.

"Great. So, Jack Frost, the owner of the children's toy store, while dressed as Santa Claus, gets drunk at the Christmas party and drowns. That will only give them more ammunition." I point out.

Of course, I pity him and his friends and family when they find out he died. Especially so close to Christmas. But I also hate the idea of a bunch of busybodies trying to overregulate alcohol in Crested Peaks.

Many of our small businesses rely heavily on the tourists who come here to ski and enjoy our picture-postcard town. If they couldn't enjoy a beer with dinner while they're here, they'd go elsewhere, I'm sure of it.

"His name isn't really Jack Frost, is it?" Miranda asks.

"I always wondered that myself," Damien chimes in. "I assume it isn't. Or his parents named him that, and what could he do but become a toy store owner."

"Is he from Crested Peaks? Does his family live here?" I ask the group, but I'm met only with blank looks. "I remember the toy store when I was younger, and how he played Santa for all the kids at Christmas every year, but that's about it."

"This will be an enormous blow to the town. Everybody loved him and looked forward to his enchanted decorations and all the cool toys his store had." Tom says.

"This is going to look so bad when word gets out. Crested Peaks beloved Santa drowns at the annual Christmas party," I moan. "Am I a horrible person that I worry about that?" I ask. "I feel awful that he died that way. It's heartbreaking to think of someone drinking too much, then going for a walk to get some fresh air. They slip out a back door completely unnoticed only to die alone in the dark waters of the Glacier Lake." Everyone nods their heads in silence. "But I also worry about what seems like non-stop bad news to come out of Crested Peaks lately. It was only last month that the reporter from Los Angeles nearly ruined us all."

"I completely hear what you're saying, Char," Drew says, giving me a comforting squeeze. "The police station has been inundated with calls ever since Evelyn Lawson's meltdown live on tv."

"Who's calling you?" Miranda asks.

"You name it, they're calling. Reporters, politicians, tourists, the list goes on. Some of them call with advice, and others want to know if the rumors are true, tv stations want to interview us. It's crazy."

"Once again it's been a memorable evening everyone, but we need to head out, assuming you don't need us for anything," Damien informs the group. "The babysitter has to get home, and you and I have an early morning tomorrow," he reminds me.

"You're right. O'dark thirty doesn't come in the middle of the afternoon, does it? It looks like everyone else is headed home, too. Nothing like another dead body to clear out the room!"

Chapter Three

Driving to work the following morning, the rabbits are full of questions about the party the night before.

"That wasn't the real Santa they found floating in the lake, right?" Marshall asks.

"No, it was the owner of the toy store, Jack Frost."

"The toy store is boring," Marcus informs us.

"Why would you call a toy store boring?" I ask.

"There's no treats!" they answer in unison.

"Oh, right. What about you, Stumpy? You play with toys, right?"

"He says they don't have cat toys there. Only human toys." Marcus answers for him.

It was hard to get used to the talking rabbits at first. When I was a kid, Gran insisted the rabbits talked to her, but I always wondered if she was pulling my leg. Everybody thinks their pets talk to them, right?

At the same time, I secretly wanted animals to talk to me too, though. The first time I heard the rabbits talking directly to me after she died, I nearly had a heart attack.

They also nearly gave Damien a heart attack at Thanksgiving when he realized that his foster daughter, Poppy could talk to not just Marshall and Marcus like I can, but Stumpy too. That was also when Damien found out Poppy is a witch.

It's not that he's opposed to witches or talking animals. He worked for my grandma for years, after all. But he's not always sure how to handle it. He was relieved to learn that their dog Bubbles doesn't talk. Not even to the rabbits or Stumpy. Which the rabbits consider unnatural. Leave it to an enchanted rabbit to decide a dog that doesn't talk is unnatural.

When we pull into the parking lot, I notice Damien is already there, as usual. The warm lights of the cafe reflect onto the dark street, and a gentle snow drifts down. I look up at the wooden sign that hangs over the cafe and smile. This hasn't been the easiest year ever, but I have come to love this town and the friends I've made here.

It frustrates me that outsiders may judge us because of the sensational stories that have been told about us recently. If only they knew it's a great town. During the holidays, it looks exactly like the movies you see at Christmas time, except our snow is real and the trees in the background aren't suspiciously green and full of leaves.

Shopkeepers' Christmas lights twinkle up and down Main Street, and everything looks so festive. I feel horrible that Mr. Frost died the way he did. I hope they can locate his family, so they know what happened to him.

And I wonder what will happen to the toy store now. He always had the best toys. He had an enormous selection that he ordered from all over the world. Some were made locally by people who live in Crested Peaks, while others came from various parts of Colorado.

It will be a shame to lose the store, but I'm sure someone else will fill the space. Although Rita, the woman who owns the Marcall's building, still hasn't found a suitable tenant for next door. After the mob shoot out there, she's being extra picky about who leases it.

"Good morning!" Damien calls out as I let myself in the back door. The smell of freshly simmering black beans tickles my nose, and my stomach reminds me I didn't eat breakfast yet.

"Look at what I put together this morning," he says, holding a delightful-looking loaf of something in front of me.

I breathe deep. "That smells heavenly. What is it?"

"Chocolate chip eggnog bread with a brown butter glaze," he says proudly.

"I want some! I'm starving!" I tell him.

"I'll cut you off a slice right now. And coffee?"

"Do you really have to ask?" I scold him while digging into the freshly baked bread, watching the chocolate chips melt against the fork. My mouth waters before I can even take a bite.

"Any word from Drew yet?" he asks.

"Nothing new, but I'm sure we won't hear anything until they complete the autopsy."

"What a way to go," he says, shaking his head sorrowfully.

"I can't quite imagine drinking so much that I fall into an icy lake and drown," I add. When I glance up at the clock to see that it's 6:29, I leap up from the stool I'm sitting on, dash through the kitchen and into the dining area.

Gladys is always here precisely at 6:30, looking for her cup of coffee and vegan breakfast burrito. Every single morning. And if I don't unlock the door by 6:30, she knocks. This morning is no exception, and the moment I turn the lock, she's practically pulling the door out of my hands.

"Good morning, one and all!" she calls out. "What a party last night, huh?"

I nod my head, knowing what's coming next. Gladys is known as the town gossip, and she has the scoop on everything. Her nose for news has proven helpful when trying to solve a murder.

She's a tall woman with thick gray hair piled on her head and always dresses impeccably, especially for 6:30 AM. I'm lucky if I can find a clean t-shirt to put on and remember to brush my teeth this time of the morning.

Today she's wearing a massive fur hat which she assures me is fake, and a large puffy white coat that goes to her knees. Somehow, her boots match all three.

"Have you heard anything new about Jack Frost?" I ask her.

"I haven't, and what a shame. Falling into the lake and drowning in the middle of the night because you're too drunk to realize any differently," she says with a shudder. "I can't imagine."

"Do you know if he has any family in town?" I ask, certain she'll have the answer to that.

"Not as far as I know. He's kind of a loner who showed up many years ago, opened a toy store, and never left. I've never seen him with anyone or heard about him having any family. I don't even know if Jack Frost is his real name."

"We were talking about that last night. Everybody seemed to love him."

"How could you not love Santa?" Gladys asks.

"Top of the morning to you, Gladys!" Damien announces, carrying her burrito and coffee.

"Damien! How's that sweet little girl of yours?"

"She's getting more excited by the second for Christmas," he tells us. "Her grandmas have gone overboard with the presents, though. I swear the delivery guy drops off packages non-stop throughout the day. I don't know where we're going to put it all! And she still cherishes the unicorn bed you got for her, Gladys. We'll never be able to thank you enough for that."

"Oh, pish. My pleasure, deary. I'm thrilled she likes it." Gladys dismisses him with a wave of her hand. When Poppy lost her mother, she also lost her beloved bright pink and purple unicorn bed because she couldn't take it with her to the group home, she was living in.

When Tom and Damien took her in, what she wanted more than anything in the world was to have that bed back, but it was long gone. They scoured the state looking for one when, lo and behold, a bed showed up at the cafe from Gladys. Who refuses to tell us how she found it. This is why I love this town so much. People do things like that for each other without expectation. It's amazing.

After Gladys finishes her breakfast, and prepares to leave, I make her promise to let us know if she hears anything. Time drags on all morning when business is unusually slow.

"You don't think it has anything to do with what happened last night, do you?" Damien asks, concern etching his face.

"Word couldn't have gotten around that fast, could it?" I ask.

"Please. This is Crested Peaks. You bet it has."

When Aranya shows up for her shift, after a morning of classes at Colorado Mountain College, she whistles. "Oh boy, you guys, it's like a ghost town out there! Where are all the holiday shoppers?"

"Damien thinks it has something to do with Jack Frost drowning last night," I tell her.

"Were you there last night? Did you see what happened?"

"We only heard the screams, but for once, we weren't the ones who discovered the body."

"We?" Damien asks.

"Okay, I didn't find the body," I add.

"We didn't find it either!" Marcus calls out from the back.

"The rabbits didn't find it either," I tell Aranya. Last summer, we hired her to help in the cafe, and she's been fabulous. Her parents own the Thai One On food truck, and she's a culinary student at the local college.

It's been a relief to have someone else here when I have to go out. Or, as Damien puts it, when Miranda and I are out investigating crimes that we shouldn't be investigating in the first place. He doesn't have to be in the cafe all alone.

"I notice that Mrs. Schmidt and her cronies are going door to door today, too. Maybe people are hiding from them."

"Why are they going door to door?" I ask.

"They've started a petition."

"For what?" Damien asks.

"They want to ban alcohol in Crested Peaks."

I laugh until I see the look on her face. "C'mon, you must be joking."

She shakes her head. "I'm not. They said after what happened last night, it's time for Crested Peaks to go dry. They insist it will be better for the children and that there would be practically no crime if liquor is no longer allowed in the town."

"That's preposterous! They can't do that! No one would ever go along with that."

"I don't know. It looks like she has a lot of signatures on her petition. People are scared. Think about it. There were two murders a year ago, then the attempted mafia takeover last spring, then the magician's assistant stabbed at the Fourth of July Festival, then the mortician poisoned on Halloween, and then the high-profile murder of the soap opera star at Thanksgiving."

"Okay, okay, I got it!" I exclaim, waving my hands around to try and get her to stop with all the details. What she tactfully left out was that I've personally been involved with every one of those cases. And all have occurred since I've been back in town.

"What is it with holidays and murder in this town?" Damien asks.

"I don't know, and I wish I could stop hearing about it," I snap. "Besides, Mr. Frost wasn't murdered last night; he drowned because he was... oh never mind." I grumble.

Having a dry town would destroy business in this area. No one would come here to ski if they couldn't go out to dinner afterward and enjoy a glass of wine. The bars and restaurants would go broke. This could be a disaster.

I continue to grumble about all of this when who should appear but Mrs. Schmidt herself. Her petition grasped firmly in her hands.

"Hi there," she starts. "I don't think we've met, but I'm Bitsy Schmidt with the Women's Anti-Liquor Coalition."

"I know exactly who you are, and we're not signing your petition. What you're trying to do will destroy all the small businesses in this town," I snap.

"On the contrary. If we ban alcohol in Crested Peaks, the town will thrive. Business owners can convert their current businesses into healthier establishments, like smoothie bars, salad restaurants, and yoga studios. I'd think that as the owner of a vegetarian cafe, you'd be the first to sign on with our movement."

"I don't believe in telling adults what they can and can't drink on their own time," I growl at her. I can't believe they think they can get away with this.

"Well, what about the children?" she asks. "A beloved town symbol of Santa Claus and toys perished last night because he couldn't control his drinking. What will the children think when they find out Santa is dead? It's not even his fault. If he hadn't been tempted by free-flowing alcohol at the party last night, he'd be alive and opening his toy shop as we speak."

"I'm not supporting your petition. In fact, I'll oppose it with everything I've got." I glare at her, my fists jammed firmly at my hips.

"I assume you won't mind if your employees sign it, though?" she smirks.

"My employees are free to do as they choose," I tell her, and I mean it.

"Don't look at me!" Aranya exclaims, throwing her hands in the air and walking off.

"I'm with Charlotte on this one," Damien says. "Banning alcohol in Crested Peaks would be a disaster, and besides, I don't think it's appropriate."

"Stumpy says he can pee in her shoe if you want him to!" Marcus shouts from the kitchen.

"We're good, thank you!" I call back while Bitsy looks at me like I'm unhinged.

Then, as I'm hoping to get rid of her, Drew walks in.

"Detective Bailey!" she crows.

"Mrs. Schmidt." He nods at her.

"Care to sign our petition outlawing liquor in Crested Peaks?" she asks, thrusting the petition in his direction.

"I'm not allowed to sign any petition," he explains. "Department policy."

I almost laugh at her look of disdain.

"After what happened last night, in addition to the rampant crime throughout the town, I'd think the department would wholeheartedly support this measure."

"Crime is hardly rampant, Bitsy," Drew tells her.

"You have news?" I ask, leaning in on my toes. I'm so eager to find out what he knows.

"Jack Frost didn't drown because he was drunk. He had what amounted to about half of a peppermint martini in his stomach when he died, according to the coroner's office."

"Then how did he die?" I ask.

"He was murdered."

Chapter Four

"M urdered?" we all exclaim simultaneously.

"How?" I ask, my voice abnormally high-pitched. How can this be happening again?

"Someone placed flunitrazepam in his drink," Drew says calmly.

"What's flunit... um whatever," Mrs. Schmidt asks.

"Also known as a roofie," Aranya tells us while Drew points his finger at her, indicating that she's correct.

"Who would want to kill Santa?" Damien asks.

"Just when you think it couldn't get any worse," I mutter. Santa didn't just die. He was murdered. Then it occurs to me. "You said he had about half of a martini, right?" I ask.

"Yes," Drew nods his head.

I turn to Bitsy, unable to hide the triumphant look on my face. "So, he obviously wasn't drunk!"

"Nope. His blood alcohol was only .02%" Drew says.

Bitsy looks embarrassed. "Well. Even if he wasn't drunk, that's still another murder in this town. You haven't heard the last from me, I assure you."

"Bummer," Aranya whispers as she stomps out the door.

"I'm glad we got rid of her, but that's still horrible that someone would want to kill Jack. Any leads?" I ask, turning to Drew, who then eyes me narrowly. I throw up my hands. "I'm not asking because I'm investigating! I'm genuinely curious." He and Damien, both look at me like they don't believe me.

"No solid leads yet."

"When this gets out, it will be so bad for business." Aranya laments. "It was only Thanksgiving that the soap opera star was murdered, and now Santa Claus? The town is already quiet today. This can only make things worse."

"I can't stay long," Drew explains. "But I was up the street, and so I decided to stop by." He looks at Damien like he's hoping he won't have to ask.

"Donuts to go?" Damien asks.

"I thought you'd never ask!"

While Damien places some of our famous half-calorie, full taste donuts in a bag, Drew takes the time to urge me to leave the investigation to the professionals.

"We don't know who we're dealing with here, Char. It could get very dangerous, and I don't want to worry about you. Any of you," he says, pointing to each of us.

"As I already said earlier, I'm not doing that anymore. I have full confidence that the Crested Peaks Police Department is more than capable of handling this. Meanwhile, I'll keep serving up Damien's delicious food," I assure him.

"I'll keep an eye on them, Detective," Damien insists as he hands him the donuts, and I roll my eyes.

"I know I can count on you," Drew tells him.

"Keep us updated!" I shout after Drew as he leaves, happily clutching the donuts in his hand.

"You aren't serious, are you?" Aranya asks.

"About what?" I respond.

"About ignoring the fact, we have another murder to solve. It's empty out there," she says, pointing to the street. "And in case you hadn't noticed, it's empty in here too!"

"It's one of those days," I assure her. "People are busy with their holiday preparations, too. They'll be back as soon as they're finished."

Before I can say anything more, Miranda bursts through the door as she normally does when she's sure that Drew has stopped by with news.

"What did Drew have to say? Any additional news? You kicked that snake out, right? She tried to get signatures at Bean Around a Bit, but I sent her packing. The nerve of that woman. Banning alcohol in Crested Peaks. She's the one who ought to be banned. What did Drew say?" she utters in such a rush she's almost out of breath. When the three of us stare at her, wondering if she's finished her speech, she continues. "And before you ask, yes, I had an espresso. Or maybe several."

"I figured as much," I tell her. With her spiky yellow hair today and her usual non-stop chatter, she reminds me of the Tweek character from South Park."Drew said Jack Frost was murdered."

"What?" she shrieks. "How?"

"I guess someone spiked his peppermint martini?" I tell her, giving a bewildered shrug.

"Who would do such a thing?"

"I don't know, and it's none of my business."

"None of your business? Of course, it's your business! Have you noticed how quiet it is out there? It's been slow ever since Thanksgiving at my shop. If it doesn't pick up again soon, I may have to lay people off!"

"Wait, seriously? Why didn't you say something before?"

Miranda wags her head. "I didn't want to worry you, and I keep thinking that it's only a short-term slump. And that things will turn around any day now. But with another murder on our hands, I'm worried."

"I guess we've been on the slow side, too. I keep thinking it's the holidays and that people are busy doing other things. Even so, it's not up to me to solve this. The CPPD is perfectly capable of handling this. We just have to wait it out and hope for the best. They'll solve this murder soon, and things will go back to normal. You'll see."

Miranda looks skeptical. "I wish I had your optimism."

"Hey, lady!" Marshall says.

"I swear, I don't care if there's a body in the freezer. I don't want to know about it." All too often, when one of the rabbits starts a conversation with "Hey lady," it's because they've found a body.

"Why would there be a body in the freezer?" Marcus asks.

"I'm using it as an example," I explain.

Meanwhile, Marshall and Marcus look at each other like they think I'm completely off my rocker.

"Assuming there's no actual body anywhere near here, what were you going to tell me?"

"Mr. Barnes from the tobacco shop said he's closing the store."

"Why?"

"Going out of business," Marshall explains. "He said with all the negative publicity lately; the tourists are afraid to come here."

"I thought after the reality tv show was here, the ski area said they have more reservations than ever!" I remind everyone.

"The ski area is one thing, but all the shops in town are another," Miranda reminds me. "Tourists come to ski but then drive into another town nearby to do their shopping, I guess."

"I can't get involved in this. You heard me. I told Drew I wouldn't."

Damien nods his head. "Yes, you did."

"What if you put out a few feelers? Maybe ask around a bit without getting too deep into the investigation?" Aranya suggests. "See what people are talking about. After all, you said it yourself last time that people are often more forthcoming with you because you're not a cop. They're more likely to open up to you."

"You did say that," Miranda reminds me.

"I don't know you guys. I should mind my own business and stick to running a cafe."

"You may not have a cafe to run if this keeps up!" Aranya says.

"Have you forgotten already how I nearly got Damien killed last time? And you, Aranya? It's my fault we were almost burned to death in that warehouse! I don't want to put any of you at risk."

"You're making the right decision," Damien says, resting his hand on my arm to reassure me. "You're not a cop. You're a restaurant owner. Please keep your head down and stick to what you do best. Things will pick up soon. I know they will."

I catch the look between Miranda and Aranya as he says this. They're always quick to go along with my schemes, while Damien is the cautious one. But still, I can't put my friends in danger anymore. Even if it means we have to tighten the purse strings for a while until things calm down.

"I guess I should get back to the coffee shop now. Let me know if you change your mind!" Miranda tells me, sounding rather glum.

"You'll be fine. We'll all be fine." I reassure her.

I realize I may have spoken too soon when Chloe, the owner of Chloe's Cupcakes food truck, shows up and she looks like she's been crying.

"Oh, no!" I blurt out. "What's wrong?"

It was only Halloween when Chloe was accused of murdering her old boss, the town mortician, with a poisoned cupcake. "I'm leaving Crested Peaks," she says softly.

"You can't leave here! You love Crested Peaks. You've spent your whole life here. You started the cupcake business so that you could stay here. I don't understand. Why would you leave?"

"Business is terrible, Charlotte. I'll take the truck elsewhere and start over. It was bad enough that I was falsely accused of poisoning Morley, but with all the bad news lately, I can't stay here and make a living. And I feel terrible because you worked so hard to exonerate me, and then you were almost killed in the process, but if I don't start making money on the truck, I'll lose it."

"Oh, no, I'm so sorry, Chloe. Are you sure you can't hold on a little longer? Maybe things will pick up after Christmas?"

"I thought the same thing, but then someone told me that Jack Frost, the toy store owner, was murdered last night? Is that true?" she sniffles.

I hang my head. "I'm afraid so."

"See, that makes things ten times worse. Now everyone will be scared away because they think there's a killer on the loose. That settles it. I have to move, and I wanted you to hear it from me in person."

"But where will you go?" I ask. I can't believe Chloe is leaving.

"I was thinking about Grand Junction. I don't know. I have to pack everything up and find someplace to live over there. I'll come by again before I leave to say goodbye."

"I'm so sorry, Chloe. If there's anything I can do to change your mind, let me know, okay?"

"Catch Jack's killer like you have all the rest? The whole town needs that right now. I'm afraid if the killer isn't caught soon, I won't be the only one leaving."

At that, I hear Damien's sigh of resignation, and I'm sure I can hear Aranya's smile all the way across the room.

Chapter Five

"Charlotte, I know you're upset, but you need to stop and take a breath. You told Drew you'd stay out of it," Damien begs.

"It's not like I *promised* him," I emphasize. "I just said I was done with all of that. Besides, it can't hurt to stop by the toy store and see what's happening now. Maybe Mr. Frost's family will show up, and we can find out if they know anything. Perhaps he has some long-lost enemy that none of us knew about, and this will be solved before I have to do anything except ask a few questions. And who knows? He might have an angry ex-wife who has always been out to get him, and then Drew can question her, and everything can go back to normal."

"I can't talk you out of this, can I?" Damien says, scrunching up his face in frustration.

"There's nothing to talk me out of, silly. I'm going to walk over there right now and look around. I'll only be a little while."

"Fine," he sighs. "Please be careful."

I grab my coat from the hook in the kitchen and bundle myself up before heading out into the chilly winter afternoon.

Miranda and Aranya are right. This close to Christmas, the sidewalk and shops would normally bustle with activity.

Shoppers would be everywhere buying last-minute gifts, and friends with time off would meet up for hot cocoa and cookies at any of the restaurants in town. But the streets are eerily quiet today.

As I walk quietly down Main Street, I see shopkeepers peek out their windows at me, hoping that some new customers will suddenly materialize. Chloe was right. This is a disaster, and if we don't do something soon, the entire town could be in big trouble.

I pause in front of the Santa's Workshop Toy Store and peer in the window. Most of the lights are off, and the sign says closed, but I can see a young man who appears to be doing some paperwork toward the back of the store.

But as I decide to go in and say hello, I'm startled when a woman behind me barks, "They're closed!"

I whirl around, my pulse surging. I've had so many close calls lately, and now, with another murder to think about, I'm a little on edge. I'm relieved, however, when it's only a woman wearing an apron that reads Abby's Delicious Delights.

So far, she looks pretty innocent. I don't think someone wearing a bakery apron is on the prowl looking to murder a random person on the sidewalk. Although this is Crested Peaks, so who knows?

"Hi there, I was hoping to talk to someone at the toy store. Did you know the owner?"

"I'm Abby Hooper, and I own Abby's Delicious Delights," she says, pointing to the sign over the bakery next door.

"Oh, hi, I'm Charlotte Duffin, and I own Marcall's Breakfast Cafe down the street," I explain, pointing toward Marcall's.

"Yes, I've heard of you. You're the one with the rabbits who run around town with a two-footed cat following them."

"Uhhh, guilty! I hope they haven't been bothering you. I know they like to visit the shopkeepers in town and beg for treats. If it's a problem, I can tell them to stay away."

"Nah, they don't stop by here very often. I have little for rabbits. Or a cat. Although occasionally, when I'm making fruit pies, I give them a blueberry or a slice of apple."

"I'm sure they love that!" I tell her. "Do you know what they plan to do with the toy store? I see there's someone in there now doing paperwork in the back."

"That would be Will Fleming. He works, uh, *worked*, for Jack."

"So, he's not related to him or anything?"

"Nah, I know nothing about Jack's family. I don't know if he even has a family. He was pretty quiet and kept to himself a lot. I always thought it was kind of weird that he had that shop here for so many years, and yet no one knew anything about him. Most people liked him but didn't know him personally."

"You say 'most people liked him.' Are you telling me *you* didn't like him?"

Abby takes a deep breath while playing with the tie on her apron, like she's stalling. Or hiding something. "There was often a lot of what I consider suspicious activity going on around here," she starts.

"Suspicious? What do you mean by that?"

"People would come and go all the time."

"Errrr, it is a toy store?" I point out.

"No, silly, not like that. Obviously, he has customers who come and go. I mean the stuff that happens behind the scenes. Late at night and on days when the store is closed."

"I'm still not sure what you mean."

Sometimes when I'm at the bakery first thing in the morning, or late at night catching up on paperwork, I notice strange people who pull to the back door, go inside for a few minutes but then come right back out."

"But you can't tell what they're doing?" I ask.

"The backdoor is at a weird angle compared to my store," she explains, shaking her head. "I could see a car, or even the front of a car, and an outline of a person, but it was hard to see the rest. And I know that most legitimate shop owners don't have visitors at all hours like that. I certainly don't. Do you?"

"No, of course not."

"I would also see cars drive by the front very slowly all the time. Almost like they were casing it, but he never got robbed or anything." She waves her hand in front of her to mimic the cars cruising along Main Street.

"Did you ever ask him about it?"

"All the time. In fact, I even complained to the County office on more than one occasion."

"What did Jack say about it?"

"He claimed he didn't know what I was talking about. And it was my word against his, so what could I do?" she responds with a shrug.

"Do you have any security cameras installed?" I ask.

"No, it was one of those things where I kept meaning to but never actually did it. I got estimates from a few different companies but then didn't follow through. I was worried that if I installed a camera that pointed directly at his store, he'd complain to the authorities that I was violating his privacy or something."

"Do you think it was drugs?" I ponder.

"I think it's a good possibility," she says. "What else would it be? Sketchy people visiting on the off-hours, only going in for a few minutes, almost always in a car or a small SUV. Whatever they were getting from the shop had to be small, right? It's not like they were pulling up in massive delivery trucks and spending hours in the place."

"Did Jack ever report a crime?"

"Not that I know of."

"So, he knew they were there," I point out.

"I assume he's the one who opened the door for them. Especially since he denied it was happening when I saw it with my own eyes."

After that, we both fall silent, reflecting on the conversation. But she doesn't stop playing with the tie on her apron. As I try to ask her where she was the night of the party, she starts to tell me she needs to get back to the bakery. We giggle nervously over the mistake.

"You first," she says.

"I was wondering if you were at the party last night. You know, maybe you saw something suspicious that no one else saw." Yeah, I admit it, I'm a big liar. I want to know if she has an alibi. Although if she mentioned she saw something suspicious, it would be helpful.

"Nope, I was here baking," she says, pointing back at her bakery. "It's always insane this time of year. Customers decide they want things at the last minute and get all fired up when I tell them they should have reserved it in advance like everyone else."

"You get a lot of party orders?" I ask.

"I do. And my little shop is too small to handle the bigger orders. I need more ovens and space."

"That's interesting because most people are telling me that their business is down," I tell her.

She nods her head. "Foot traffic is definitely down. But orders have jumped. It's like people don't want to stroll down Main Street and stop in for a piece of pie and coffee like they used to. They've been more inclined to order a tray of cookies for the office party or a pecan pie for their family dinner."

"Oh, I see. Well, nice that you're still keeping busy, I guess."

"If you're hoping to catch whoever killed Jack, I'd have a conversation with Will if I were you," she tells me, tilting her head in his direction where he remains hard at work. I don't think he's even noticed us out here talking.

"You think he might know something about Jack's death?" I ask.

"He's worked for him for years."

"Perhaps he knows something about all the suspicious visitors that they get?" I ask.

"He always denied it to me, but I'd give it a shot if I were you."

"Okay, I will. Thanks for your time."

"Sure thing, and good luck. The last thing this town needs is for 'Santa murdered in Crested Peaks' to be the next headline."

"I hear you!" I tell her as I watch her head back to her bakery. I wonder if what she claims about the suspicious activity is true. Or is this a dispute between neighboring shop owners, and she wants to make him look bad? Or could she even be the killer? I don't know what her motive would be, but she seemed awfully quick to point out the alleged criminal activity to a total stranger.

Chapter Six

I decide it would be best to talk to Will while I'm here. Who knows when I'll get another chance like this?

I make it obvious that I'm peering into the window, hoping he'll see me. I balance my hands against the glass while pressing my nose to it. There's no way he doesn't see me.

People walking by on the sidewalk are looking at me with odd expressions. But Will doesn't even glance up. Ugh. Why can't he make this easy on me? I finally try the "Hello!" and tap on the window. He still doesn't look up; he's so engrossed in his work.

What is wrong with this guy? I bang even harder while he continues to ignore me. Now I'm annoyed. There's no way he doesn't hear me. I march over to the door and try to pull it open. He's made me more determined than ever to discuss this with him.

It's locked. Grrr! I look to the left and then the right. No one seems to be paying attention now. I suppose this is illegal, but I don't care. I'll talk to this guy if it's the last thing I do. Although given my recent runs ins with a variety of bad guys, I probably shouldn't be saying things like that to myself.

I concentrate on the lock, and it slowly slides open. I smile and give myself a mental pat on the back. When I first returned to Crested Peaks, and was still reluctant to practice witchcraft in front of anyone, unlocking a door using magic was a big deal. I was always worried I'd screw it up and embarrass myself.

Look at me now, I think. Here I am, breaking and entering without a second thought. But don't tell Drew. I slip through the door and walk quietly toward Will is working.

The store is dark except for the small desk lamp he is working under. The lamp lights up his features in an eerie glow, and I shiver as I realize this probably isn't the smartest thing I've ever done. "Excuse me," I half whisper.

He jumps from the stool he's sitting on scrambling to shove all the papers together in front of him. He quickly throws a file folder over them, but not before I see several sketches of what look like elegant and ornate watches.

"How did you get in here?" he demands. "The door was locked! I'm calling the cops!"

"Oh, the door was open! How else would I get in?" I tell him. Fortunately, it occurred to me at the last second to leave it unlocked, in case he calls my bluff. Besides, the last thing I need to do is lock myself in a toy store with a suspected killer.

"Uh, no, it's locked!" he exclaims.

"See for yourself." I point at the door. I can tell he wants to test it out, but he keeps glancing down at the stack of papers he's trying to hide. He doesn't want to leave me alone with them.

"Fine. Whatever." he grunts. "We're closed. In case you didn't hear already, the owner of the store died last night. And I'm trying to finish up some paperwork."

"You worked for Jack?" I ask.

"I did. And who are you?"

"I'm Charlotte Duffin. I own Marcall's." I turn to point in the general direction of the cafe.

"Oh yeah," he smirks. "That's where those two rabbits and the cat live."

Is there anyone who doesn't know the three of them?

"Yes, they do."

"Is there something you needed? Did you place an order or something? Because we'll still be processing any of those for Christmas, but after that, I'm not sure what will happen."

"Do you know if Jack had any family or relatives? Someone he may have left the business to?" I ask.

"I don't know," he says, swinging his head to indicate a sharp no.

"How long did you work for him?"

"About five years," he explains.

"And you don't know if he had any family?" I ask in disbelief.

"What can I say? He was a very private guy. I knew very little about him."

"I understand. Some people are like that. I was passing by the bakery, and Abby mentioned she saw a lot of what she considered suspicious activity here. Do you know anything about that?"

Will narrows his eyes and stares at me. "She's lying."

"Why would she lie about something like that?"

"You'll have to ask her. She was always whining about it and even filed a complaint with the county. She's crazy."

"So, you're saying it isn't true?" I press.

"If suspicious people showed up here as often as she claims they did, I knew nothing about it," he says. However, I don't believe him for a second.

"Were you at the party last night when he died?"

"Why?" he says in such a clipped way it startles me.

"I was just curious. I thought if you were, maybe you saw something suspicious, that's all."

"I was at the movies with my girlfriend."

"Oh, that's nice. What did you see? I'm always looking for a good movie."

"I'm not sure," he says.

"You went to the movies last night, but you aren't sure what you saw? It was only a day ago."

"I didn't mean that. I meant I can't remember the name of it."

"Oh, I see. Was it a comedy?"

"No, I don't think so," he responds. This guy is getting more suspicious by the second.

"A romance? I bet your girlfriend likes romantic movies, doesn't she?"

"Oh yeah, she does. It was definitely a romantic movie."

"Oh!" I snap my fingers. "Was it that new Nicholas Sparks movie?"

"Yeah, that was it. It was good too."

"Good to know. I'll have to check it out myself."

"You should. Hey, I don't mean to be rude or anything, but I have a lot of work to do here," he explains.

"I'm sorry to have bothered you. I was wondering what will happen to the toy store now that Mr. Frost is dead."

"I suppose that will be for the lawyers to decide. I don't know how things like this work. But really quick, before you go. If you're looking for people to ask about who might have killed Jack, you should talk to Scarlett Wise."

"Who's Scarlett Wise?" I ask.

"She was suing Jack because she claimed he stole one of her toy inventions."

"No way! Was it worth a lot of money?"

Will whistles. "Lady, it was worth a boatload of money. Jack was set to sell it to Jay Bee Toy Company."

"That's huge."

"And Scarlett was furious. Here, I have one of the emails she sent him recently." He opens a drawer and hands me a printed copy of an email from Scarlett, and *yikes* is all I can think to say. It was an angry tirade full of expletives, and the last sentence says *I'll get you when you least expect it.*

"Do you mind if I keep this?"

"No problem," he says. "I can print out another one of the police want it."

"Thanks!" I nod my head at him, waving the printed email around. Now I need to find Scarlett.

Chapter Seven

As I head back toward Marcall's, I decide to do the right thing and stop at the police station first to see if Drew is in. I seem to get in slightly less trouble, and I do mean slightly, when I let him know what I'm doing rather than simply running around town investigating crimes without consulting him.

And yes, I realize I already tracked down two witnesses before telling him, but, whatever. I'm at least trying, and that's what counts, right? I text Damien to let him know I'll be out a while longer because I'm stopping by the police station first.

He'll be happy about that, too. I stop at the front desk to check in with Sargeant Pratt. "Hey there, Charlotte! How's it going? Here to see Detective Bailey, I assume?"

"Hi, Sargeant, and yes, is he around?"

"I think so; let me double check."

She buzzes Drew at his desk. "Detective, Charlotte is here to see you."

Within a matter of seconds, Drew races to the front. "Charlotte! What are you doing here? Is everything okay?"

"Yeah, it's fine. I just wanted to stop by and talk to you for a monent if you aren't too busy."

"Of course not, come on back. What's going on? Is everybody all right? Did something happen?"

I look askance. "Can't I stop in to see my handsome boyfriend once in a while?" I ask.

"You've never stopped in to see me," he says, looking at me blankly.

"Oh, yeah, good point. In the effort of full disclosure, I wanted to tell you what I discovered today before you hear it from someone else."

"Uh oh," he says, pointing to the chair next to his desk. "You promised me you wouldn't get involved in this."

I hold up my finger. "Now, to be fair, I didn't really promise. I just said I was done with all of that."

"Go on," Drew sighs so loudly several of his co-workers turn to look at him with amused looks on their faces. They're undoubtedly aware of his trials and tribulations where investigations and his girlfriend are concerned.

"I walked over to the toy store to see if anything was happening there yet."

"And..." he prompts me.

"I was peering in the window, and Abby, the baker from next door, came out to talk to me."

As I say that, Drew flips through his notebook to consult with what he's already recorded. "I have nothing on her," he tells me.

"She mentioned that she often saw sketchy looking people, as she called them, showing up at the toy store at all hours of the night and when they were closed."

"Hang on a second," he says, typing at the computer. "Yes, we have several complaints from her about that. But she could never prove that these so-called sketchy people were showing up and cruising by the store all the time. When we questioned Jack Frost about it, he always insisted he didn't know what she was talking about. It went no further. Do you think she's telling the truth?"

"What reason does she have to make something like that up?" I point out.

"Your guess is as good as mine," Drew says.

"I asked her where she was when Jack was killed."

"I'm sure she loved that," Drew says, almost like he's trying not to laugh.

"I didn't say it like that, obviously, but she said she was working at the bakery trying to get all her Christmas orders filled."

"As much as I appreciate your coming to me with this, I'm not sure what the point is. And I would still say you shouldn't be looking into this at all, but I know that's probably pointless."

"I feel like it's something you should know. Just in case."

"Anything else?"

"Welllll," I stall.

"I knew there had to be something else."

"She told me if I was looking into people who could have killed Jack that I should talk to Will Freeman."

"An employee at Santa's Workshop."

"Right."

Drew fiddles with the pen in his hands, and I can tell he's annoyed now. "You definitely shouldn't be talking to him."

I lean forward in anticipation. "Does that mean he's a suspect?"

"I didn't say that, but obviously, anyone who worked for Frost is someone we want to talk to. However, I was just there, and it didn't look like he was in."

"When I stopped by, he was in the back of the store working with all the lights out except for a desk lamp. And the door was locked."

"And he let you in?"

"Welll..."

"Charlotte!" he exclaims, throwing his pen down on the desk, causing the others to look over at us again. "Do I honestly need to remind you how many close calls you've had lately?"

"Er, no," I mumble, fidgeting with the plant on his desk. "But I have what I think is some important information."

He holds his hand up. "Don't tell me how you got in there. I don't want to know."

"Okay, I won't, but I need to tell you what Will said."

"Fine, go ahead." He slides his hands down his face and I can tell he's losing patience.

"First of all, he complained about Abby insisting something was going on at the toy shop. So, I'm still wondering if there's a problem between the two stores that we don't know about."

"And second of all?"

"I asked him where *he* was last night. And he said he was at the movies with his girlfriend. But when I asked him for details, he got cagey and couldn't even tell me what movie he saw."

Drew frowns.

"What?" I ask.

"The movie theater is temporarily closed. One of the popcorn machines caught fire and burned a huge hole in the wall."

"Ah ha! I knew he was lying!" I exclaim as Drew scribbles something in his notepad. "Plus, he told me he saw a Nicholas Sparks movie and there isn't one in theaters right now."

He looks up at me. "And third of all?"

"How did you know there was a third of all?" I ask.

"There's always a third of all with you."

"He said someone named Scarlett Wise was suing Jack because he stole her toy design, which is worth a ton of money." I pull the email out of my pocket and slide it toward him.

Drew reads over it, his forehead wrinkling with concern.

"He gave you this?" he asks.

"Yep," I nod my head, thinking he'll be pleased with it.

Instead, he waves it in the air. "This is why I don't like you getting involved in these things. You put yourself, and everyone you care for, at risk."

"But it's important, right?"

"Yes, it's important, but you have to let me follow up with it. Don't chase down Scarlett to question her, okay?"

"Okay," I admit, albeit slowly.

"Why don't I believe you?"

This time I'm the one to sigh loudly. "Fine," I grumble.

"Fine, what?"

"Fine, I won't go after Scarlett and hound her about the email."

"Thank you," he says. "And I will admit that you've brought me some important information, and as much as I hate that you went out to get this on your own, this could be helpful to our case."

"Good." I grin at him as I stand up to leave.

"Where are you going now?" he asks, his voice heavy with suspicion.

"I'm going back to work. I swear!" I hold my hand up to show him how serious I am. But I pause again before leaving. "I hope you realize that I didn't go over to the toy store just to annoy you. I'm really worried about what's happening to our town. Business is so bad that Chloe is leaving, the tobacco shop is closing, and Miranda is about the lay people off. People are afraid to go out and shop. Our entire town could be at stake here."

Drew's face softens. "I understand that you're worried and I promise you I'm doing everything I can to catch the killer."

"That's all I ask," I tell him.

Chapter Eight

When I return to Marcall's, I'm dismayed to see it's still empty. While business fluctuates throughout the day, with our busiest time being in the morning, it's rarely completely empty at this time of day.

"We've had one customer since you left," Damien informs me, as if he's reading my mind.

"One?" I gulp. That's so bad.

"Did you learn anything good, boss? And what were you doing stopping at the police station?"

"I talked to Abby," I explain, hanging my coat on the hook in the kitchen and holding my cold hands over the gas stove to warm them up.

"Abby Hooper at the bakery?" Aranya asks.

"Yes, and she mentioned that she often noticed strange people coming and going from the toy store at strange hours."

"What did Drew think of that?" Damien asks.

"He said they have a record of her complaining about it, but since Mr. Frost denied it, and Abby didn't have proof that it was happening, it went nowhere."

"Why do I think there's a but, coming?" Damien asks.

I think he's been hanging out with Drew too much. "I also talked to Will, one of the toy store employees, and he denied it ever happened as well."

"I get the sense you don't believe him, though," Aranya says.

"It seems like a weird thing to lie about. I'm not sure what she has to gain by making up stories about something like that."

"I know!" Marcus exclaims as he and Marshall hop out of my office, where they no doubt have spent the morning napping. Stumpy hobbles out right after them like always.

"And how do you know?" I turn to the three of them.

"Kyle told us." Here we go again. Whenever they have something to tell me, it always comes out in bits and pieces.

"Who's Kyle?"

"She's a feral cat who lives behind the bakery."

"And what did she tell you?"

"She said the lady who runs the bakery wants to take over the toy store," Marcus tells me.

"Why would she want to take over the toy store?" I ask.

The three of them shrug their shoulders at each other.

"Who wants to take over the toy store?" Damien asks.

"Marcus says that a cat named Kyle, who lives behind the bakery, heard that Abby wants to take over the toy store."

Damien pauses to think. "Is it the toy store or that space that she wants to take over?"

"Yes, that's it," Marshall tells me.

I nod at Damien to show he's correct.

"But would that be worth killing over?" I ponder.

"Kyle said that Abby said that she could triple her business if she could expand and that she was determined to get Jack Frost out of the way if it was the last thing she did."

"Are you absolutely certain about this?" I ask him. "This all seems a little too convenient." I point out as they shrug their tiny rabbit shoulders at me again.

Damien and Aranya patiently wait for me to tell them what the rabbits said. By now, they're used to the rabbits telling me things, and I have to fill everyone else in. Except sometimes, I get so involved in talking with the rabbits that I forget no one else can hear them.

"Abby claimed she could triple her business if she could have the toy store space."

"That's a lot." Aranya agrees.

"I assume you asked her where she was last night?" Damien says.

"She said she was at work baking Christmas orders."

"And it would be hard to prove otherwise," Aranya points out.

"Unless someone saw her, you're right," I agree. "Have you heard anything more from Miranda?" I ask them as they both shake their heads no.

"She was stressed out earlier about business being so slow. I think I'll pop over there and see how she's doing since we're not exactly slammed right now."

When I walk into Bean Around a Bit, I'm disheartened to see there's only a couple of people in there. Normally, it would be packed this time of day. I'm surprised and pleased to see her boyfriend Miles is one of the two people in the shop. He's usually hard at work in the town library right now.

"Check this out," Miranda says, holding the afternoon edition of the Crested Peaks Tribune out for me to see.

Santa found dead in Crested Peaks, the headline blares.

I start to skim the article, but I'm too depressed to continue. This is the worst. I fill her in on what I learned from my interviews this morning and what Marshall and Marcus told me.

"Ah ha! I knew it!" she shouts with glee. "I knew you couldn't stay away from this."

"After Chloe said she was leaving Crested Peaks--"

"--Chloe is leaving Crested Peaks?" she gasps.

"If she doesn't, she's worried she'll have to close her cup-cake truck because business is so bad."

"We have to do something, Char. We have to figure out who killed Santa."

"I've been working on it this morning."

"But we have to do more."

"I don't suppose you know where we can find Scarlett Wise."

"I do," Miles says.

We both turn to him in shock. "How do you know where to find Scarlett?" I ask. "I don't even know who she is."

"She's in the library all the time researching patent law," he tells us.

"Because she's suing Jack Frost," Miranda says.

"Or *was*," I remind them.

"Do you have her address?" Miranda asks him.

"I can have someone look it up. It will only take a moment." Miles assures us.

Miranda and I wait patiently while Miles calls the library to get Scarlett's address. I'm still not convinced that Abby wanting to expand into the toy store area is a motive to kill, but I definitely haven't ruled her out yet.

And there's still her claim that strange people visit the toy shop at suspicious hours. What if she's saying that because she was trying to damage Frost's reputation or something? Per-haps she thought if people suspected him of doing something illegal, she could get that space.

We already know that Will is lying for sure, and I'm hoping that we can get more details from Scarlett on the lawsuit. If it's worth a lot of money, it could give her motive.

"Here's her address," Miles says, hanging up his phone. "But don't," he adds, holding the address out of reach, "tell Drew I got this for you."

"My lips are sealed," Miranda tells him, snatching the paper from his fingers.

"But what reason will we give her for showing up at her house?" I ask.

"Donuts!" Miranda exclaims. "Donuts and coffee! How can anyone argue with someone who shows up with sweet treats?"

"It's worth a shot," I shrug.

Chapter Nine

After gathering the donuts and coffee, Miranda and I drive to Scarlett's house, which isn't quite close enough to walk, especially in the dead of winter.

We pull up in front of her house, and I turn to Miranda. "What excuse are we going to use for bringing a total stranger donuts and coffee?"

"Leave that to me," she informs me.

Uh oh. This ought to be interesting.

We ring the doorbell and just when we think she may not be home, she cracks the door open. "Can I help you with something?"

"Hi, Scarlett, I'm Miranda and this is my colleague, Charlotte. We're with the Crested Peaks Tribune and we wanted to ask you some questions about Jack Frost. We assume you're aware that he died?"

"I am," she says cautiously.

"We understand that you were involved in a lawsuit and we're doing a story on him. And we brought donuts!" Miranda says holding up the sweet snacks.

I can't believe she told her we're reporters. But thankfully, Scarlett seems interested.

"Jack Frost, or whatever his true name was, stole my idea for a computerized reading dog," she says as she lets us into her house.

"I've never heard of such a thing!" I exclaim.

"That's because I invented it! It's for kids who have trouble reading. They can read out loud to the dog and he's programmed to respond in certain ways. He can even help them sound out words and all that."

"That sounds so neat!" Miranda tells her.

"I take it you don't know his real name either?" I ask. "Assuming his real name wasn't Jack Frost."

"My lawyers are looking into it, but they're convinced that isn't his real name either. Who would be, right?"

"Why do you think he stole the idea for the dog from you?" Miranda asks.

"Because I was in there one day shopping, and I foolishly mentioned it to him. I thought, hey, here's a sweet old man who has owned this toy store forever and plays Santa Claus every year for the town's children.

"I bet he could help me bring my design to market. Maybe he even knows people who would be willing to invest. How dumb could I be? I explain the entire concept to him, and next thing I know, I see the reading dog in the store and the guy who works there--"

"--Will Fleming." Miranda fills in.

"Yeah, Will. After I ask him what my toy is doing in the store, and he says that Jay Bee Toys, that big toy manufacturer, is currently negotiating with Jack to purchase the rights to the toy and take it worldwide. I was stunned. It's worth millions, and he stole it from me."

"Do you have proof that you designed the toy first?" Miranda asks.

"You bet I do!" she announces. "My lawyers think I have an excellent case."

"Were you at the party last night?" I ask. "I'm wondering if you noticed anything suspicious," I add before she gets too suspicious of me. Considering we're already suspect in her eyes, I assume. We randomly show up with coffee and donuts, having never met her before, and claim to be reporters. Nothing weird about that at all. It's a good thing she didn't ask for ID.

"I was there at first, but after a while, I developed a horrible migraine, so I came home. I called a ride share service, and that's my proof I wasn't there when Frost was killed. In case you were interested."

"Oh, that's too bad. Migraines are the worst," I tell her, wishing I could get a psychic read on her like I do some people, but I'm not getting anything on her. I haven't sensed anything with Abby or Will, and it's frustrating. This whole situation is frustrating. I feel like whoever killed Santa is constantly one step ahead of us, and we're spinning our wheels in the mud trying to play catch up.

After thanking her for her time and promising to let her know when the story runs in the newspaper, Miranda, and I head out to the car.

In the car, Miranda turns to me. "Do we believe her? Any kind of psychic read?"

"Nothing." I shake my head sadly. "I'd say that if you think someone stole millions of dollars from you, it's enough motive to kill. But is he worth more dead or alive?"

"With him dead, I'd think it would be easier for her to get her idea back and approach the toy companies herself, don't you think?" Miranda asks.

"It seems like it, doesn't it? And still weirder that even her lawyers don't know his real name. Assuming it isn't Jack Frost."

"He's been at that toy store so long, maybe he changed it decades ago and no one remembers his real name," she suggests.

When my phone rings, I groan. "It's Drew."

"Uh oh! Do you think he knows we're here?"

"I guess we'll soon find out," I tell her.

"Hey, honey!" I chirp, hoping I don't sound too guilty.

"Hey, you're never going to believe this," he says.

Miranda mouths "*well?*"

I shrug back at her.

"We ran a background check on Will. For the last two years, he's been getting monthly payments from Jack Frost."

"Monthly payments? His paycheck?"

"No, he gets that from the Santa's Workshop Toy Store every two weeks."

"You're saying Jack Frost makes monthly payments to him personally?" I ask out loud for Miranda's benefit.

"To the tune of $5,000."

"What?" I shriek. "That's a lot of money for working at a toy store."

"We're on our way to pick up Will now, and I wanted to let you know you should avoid the toy store area if you were planning to go that direction for any reason."

"I'm staying right where I am," I tell him. Hoping he doesn't know exactly where I am.

"Just double-checking. I'll let you know if we learn anything else."

"Okay, I'll talk to you later."

"Copy," he says before hanging up. He's so weird.

When I click the phone off, Miranda throws her hands in the air. "Well?" she demands.

"Jack Frost has been paying Will Fleming $5,000 a month for the last two years - in addition to his regular paycheck."

"And you said you thought he was extra sketchy."

"Compared to Abby and Scarlett, who I only *think* are hiding something, I *knew* Will was lying to me, but I didn't know it was secret payments!"

"You think they're secret?"

"Why would Frost pay him like that out of his personal account? Drew said his paychecks came from Santa's Workshop toys every two weeks."

"This is huge, Char! What if they can get Will to crack and admit he killed Santa. That way instead of people thinking that some random killer is on the loose in Crested Peaks, they'll be relieved to know it was a disgruntled employee instead.

"Maybe Wil was even running a con job. Either way, people won't have to worry about whether it's safe to come here, and we can finally get back to normal around here. I won't have to lay people off."

"And Chloe won't have to leave town!" I add.

"Did Drew say if he had him in custody yet?"

"No, they're headed to the toy store right now. That's why he called. He didn't want me on the scene in case I had a notion to go there and talk to Will again myself."

"Instead, you're nowhere near the toy store!" Miranda exclaims.

"Exactly." I nod my head and smile.

When Miranda and I get back to our respective businesses, I'm hoping that somehow miraculously, Drew will have brought Will in already and business would be picking up, but alas, police work never seems to work that quickly.

This is one of my frustrations with it and why I often feel the need to jump in and help. But I feel even worse when I get a text from Drew

Will is in the wind. If you see him, don't approach him. Call me immediately.

Wow. I can't decide if that makes me feel better or worse. On the one hand, it confirms my suspicions about him, and once they catch him, it could help turn things around. On the other hand, what if they don't catch him, and it only makes things worse?

Because it's almost closing time anyway, and we've barely had a customer all afternoon, I send Damien and Aranya home, collect the boys, and head home. Hopefully, things will look a lot better tomorrow.

Chapter Ten

The next morning as I head into the cafe, even the twinkling Christmas lights don't cheer me up. If they don't catch Will soon and business doesn't pick up, this town is in serious trouble.

Drew texted late last night to tell me they still haven't found him. I've been racking my brain trying to figure out a way to locate Will, but I can't think of anything.

"Hey, boss!" Damien exclaims as the boys, and I walk in the back door. "Any news?"

"I don't think so," I shake my head vigorously. "Last I heard from Drew; they still hadn't found Will."

"Do you really think that Will killed Santa?"

"I know he lied to me, and Jack was making large payments in his bank account for two years. And now that the police are looking for him, he's nowhere to be found. So yeah, I think he's guilty of something, that's for sure."

"You probably don't want to look at this morning's headlines then," Damien cautions.

I groan. "What now?"

He pushes the newspaper toward me as I glance down. I know it's kind of weird that I still get a newspaper when almost everybody else gets their news on the internet. But my customers enjoy looking at the newspaper over their breakfast. But if business doesn't improve soon, I won't have any customers to read the newspaper, anyway.

Another Murder in Crested Peaks. Is the CPPD Asleep on the Job?

I bury my head in my hands. "Drew will be furious when he sees that," I whisper.

Gladys shows up for her daily 6:30 breakfast burrito like clockwork. Good ol' Gladys. She tells us that the Five Dachshund Bakery decided to close until after the New Year. They aren't getting enough business to make it worthwhile right now but they're hoping things will calm down by then and business will pick up.

Business is still slow for us and it's freaking me out. It would break my heart to have to close the café. And what would become of Damien and Aranya? It makes me nauseous to even ponder it.

About mid-morning, it stops snowing for a while, and the sun comes out. In Colorado, it isn't unusual to have it snow several inches overnight, but by morning, the sun shines brightly, melting the snow. We like to call it Mother Nature's snowplow.

"Hey, lady!" Marshall says to me after squeezing in the back door when Damien opens it to take the trash out. I didn't even realize they had gone outside.

"What now?" I grumble. "And where are Marcus and Stumpy, by the way?"

"They're looking at the man out front."

"What man?" I ask.

"The man lying on the sidewalk."

"Oh, you have got to be kidding me!" I exclaim.

"No, I'm not kidding," Marshall says. "We just found him. He's lying on the sidewalk next door. Tony's old place."

Why? Why do they do this to me? I sprint for the front door with Marshall at my heels. "I don't know if he's dead or not. There's some blood, but not as much blood as the other bodies we've found."

These three have the strangest knack for finding bodies that no one else seems to find. Although given the lack of foot traffic right now, it makes sense they'd be the ones to find somebody.

I throw open the door and see Marcus and Stumpy sitting next to a man lying face down on the sidewalk in front of the vacant storefront next door. I rush over to discover Will, who appears to have a nasty gash on the back of his head. But he doesn't look like he's been here long.

I think he's still breathing, too, because there's a little melted spot on the sidewalk in front of his mouth. I call 911 to request an ambulance. Every time I have to do this, I wonder if they're curious about why I seem to call them at least once a month.

And every time it's because I've somehow come across another person lying passed out on the sidewalk after being attacked. I swear if the animals could call themselves, I'd have them do it instead. After I hang up with the 911 call center, I quickly ring Drew.

"I found Will!" I shout before he can even say hello.

"Charlotte, please tell me you aren't at the toy store!"

"No! Marshall, Marcus, and Stumpy found him lying on the sidewalk next door to Marcall's!"

"Again?" he asks.

I seriously consider hanging up on him for that when he says, "I'll be right there. Don't touch anything."

"The ambulance is on its way too," I blurt out, but it's too late. He's already hung up. Does he just naturally assume that the boys have found another body and doesn't ask if he's even alive?

Damien then peeks his head out the door. "Hey, boss, what are--holy cheese and potatoes; what happened?"

"Quick! Grab my jacket so I can keep him warm until the ambulance comes."

Damien sprints to the kitchen and back out to where we're kneeling over Will in record time. He brought both our coats that I place over him. The sound of the ambulance siren pierces the air and I realize I'm getting a little tired of hearing that noise.

Aside from the other night, the last time I heard it was a few weeks ago when Damien was assaulted and left for dead behind Marcall's. And now, onlookers are gathering around on the sidewalk, eager to see what all the commotion is about.

I can only imagine what this will do for business. The ambulance and Drew arrive at almost the same time. Drew rushes over to us. "What happened?" he asks. "Wait, he's alive?"

"Barely, I think," I tell him as I explain how the animals found him.

"I don't think anybody had him in the pool," Damien mutters as I shoot him a salty look.

"But does it count if he's still alive?" I ask.

"No, it definitely needs to be a dead body," Damien responds.

As they load Will into the ambulance, Drew instructs the police officers who came with him to secure the area so they can search for clues.

"You didn't touch anything, right?" Drew asks.

"Nope. By now, I know exactly how all of this works. Aside from the coats we placed over him to keep him warm until the ambulance arrived, I didn't touch anything."

"Good job. I'll go to the hospital and see what I can find out about Will. You two stay here while my officers investigate the area."

"Let us know as soon as you know something."

"Of course." Drew nods his head at me and strides back to his car.

Damien sighs as we pick up our coats, and head back into Marcall's. "Another day, another guy on the sidewalk."

Chapter Eleven

I tell an officer I know that Damien and I will be inside of Marcall's if they need to ask us any questions. As much as we'd love to stand there and watch them in action, the last thing I want is to interfere. They process the scene quickly, pack up their things, and leave without asking us anything more.

"If Will didn't kill Mr. Frost, who did?" Damien asks.

"And why do they need to kill Will too?" I ponder. "Something doesn't add up here. Frost was a quiet guy who kept to himself. He seemed well-loved by most people around here - unless you thought he stole your multi-million-dollar toy idea of course."

"Or that his store was the only thing that was keeping you from expanding your business," Damien adds.

"And then there's Will, who's obviously lying *and* who is the target of the real killer, I assume. So much for getting this solved quickly. We're right back to where we started."

Damien and I are so excited when an actual customer comes through the door that we don't notice that Marshall, Marcus, and Stumpy followed him in. The three of them wait patiently while I serve the customer, but then I notice that Stumpy has something shiny in his mouth.

"What's in your mouth?" I ask.

"He found it across the street," Marcus explains.

I bend down as Stumpy drops a watch into my hand. A very expensive-looking watch. A watch that looks a lot like the sketches Will was trying to hide from me.

"Where did you get this?" I demand.

"We told you, we found it across the street," Marshall says.

"But where across the street?"

"It was lying on the sidewalk."

I hold the watch up to Damien. The crystal on the face is broken, as is the clasp. It looks like it was wrenched from someone's wrist. "This looks a lot like one of the sketches that Will covered up after I saw them."

"Do you think the killer dropped it when he attacked Will?" Damien asks.

"I think it's possible." I turn back to the animals. "This is super important, you three. Show me exactly where you found this."

"Why didn't the police see it when they were here?" Damien asks.

"It was mostly buried. But there was a piece of it sticking out in the snow," Marcus tells me. "Stumpy had to dig the rest of it up." I look across the street and notice that the sidewalk plow came through recently.

If the watch was dropped in the middle of the sidewalk, the plow may have pushed it to the side and covered it. The police probably didn't even think to look over there.

"Let's go. Show me where you dug this up," I tell them as the five of us troop out the door and across the street, leaving a bewildered diner staring at us.

I can only imagine what we look like. Two people following a pair of rabbits and a two-footed cat. While the one person acts like she's having a legitimate conversation with them.

Welcome to Crested Peaks! The animals lead us across the street, and Stumpy stares at the spot where he dug up the watch.

"I'm convinced this is the same watch, Damien. What if it has fingerprints on it?" I ask, holding it up to him.

"Besides yours?" he asks.

I nearly drop it back in the snow when I realize I've been handling it the whole time. And it's been in Stumpy's mouth.

"Drew will kill me when he finds out I touched it."

"To be fair, you didn't know what Stumpy had in his mouth right away."

"I better fess up as soon as I can," I admit. I try calling Drew, but it goes straight to voice mail. I assume he's in the hospital right now. Maybe we'll get lucky, and Will is fine and talking.

Perhaps he's admitting he knows who the killer is right this second, and it won't matter that my fingerprints are all over a piece of evidence. I text Drew instead, to let him know I think Stumpy found a piece of evidence, and that he should come by Marcall's to pick it up.

I put my hand on Damien's shoulder. "You won't like this, but I'm going over to the toy store right now."

"Char," he warns.

"This is important. I have to see if those sketches are still there."

"You mean you're breaking and entering."

"I'm going to look at the desk and see if the sketches are there. If they are, I'll contact Drew right away. I swear I won't touch anything!"

"I obviously can't talk you out of this," Damien sighs.

"That's exactly right." I pat his shoulder and head down the street. "Take the boys back to the cafe and make sure no one touches the watch until the police can pick it up!" I wave at him as I hurry away.

When I get to the toy store, I'm surprised to see a man who appears to be doing paperwork at the counter in the back. Just like Will was doing yesterday. Only all the lights are on, and the door is unlocked this time.

Ha! I think. I don't have to break in this time, and I'll simply talk to whoever that is at the desk. Maybe the store already has a new owner.

"Hello!" I call out.

The man looks cross. "Can I help you with something?"

"My name is Charlotte Duffin, and I own Marcall's Breakfast Cafe up the street."

"And?" he asks.

I glance around, hoping to see the sketches again, but the desk is clear of everything except whatever this man is working on. Which mostly appears to be a bunch of boring numbers.

"I was walking by and noticed you in here and thought I'd make sure everything was all right. I was a friend of Jack's, you see."

Sometimes it scares me how easily these made-up excuses seem to come to me on the fly.

"Oh, yes, of course. I'm Leo Price, the lawyer for Jack Frost's estate. I'm here to start the process to close the store."

"I see. Do you think you could answer a question for me?"

"Probably not."

This guy is a basket of kittens, isn't he?

"I have to know, was Jack Frost his real name?"

The lawyer pauses mid-scribble to look up at me. He glares at me over the bifocals perched on his nose. "I'm sure you realize that anything my client has told me over the years is confidential."

"Ohhh, yeah." Now I feel silly as he goes back to making notes on the paper he's working on.

"But can I ask you another question?"

He pauses his scribbling without looking up and sighs. He drops his pen on the desk crossing his arms over his chest in annoyance.

"What."

"We're aware--"

"We?" he asks.

"Um, *I'm* aware that Mr. Frost was paying his employee, Will Fleming, $5,000 each month from his personal bank account, which even you have to admit is unusual, right? Do you know why that is?"

I'm not sure I expect him to answer me. If his real name is confidential, he'll never tell me why Frost was giving Will money on the side, but I kind of want to see if he has a reaction or if my on-again off-again psychic abilities finally kick in, and I can get a read on him.

Unfortunately, it's a big nope to either of them. Mr. Price doesn't even flinch. "What Mr. Frost did with his money is no business of mine. Yours either," he lectures me, uncrossing his arms and returning to his work.

"Can I get your card real quick, if you don't mind?" I ask, now worried he'll call the cops on me or something. That's the last thing I need is for Drew to find me here harassing Jack's attorney.

He reaches into the breast pocket on his suit jacket, pulls out a card, and hands it to me without even looking up. I look at the card: Leo Price, Attorney at Law, Smithsons Law Firm.

"Thank you for your time. Sorry to have bothered you."

I almost gasp in protest when Mr. Price flicks his hand at me dismissively, like I'm a fly buzzing around his head. But as I'm about to leave, Abby comes in.

"Oh, hi Charlotte. I saw the light on in here and decided I should see what's up. Is everything okay?"

Mr. Price sighs extra loudly this time. I bet he isn't used to constantly being pestered by small-town busybodies with a bunch of questions.

"That's Leo Price, Jack Frost's attorney. He says he's here to start the process to close up the store."

"Really?" Abby asks as her eyes light up.

"Before I forget, is it true that you're hoping to expand into this store?" I ask.

She looks shocked that I know this, but she recovers quickly. "Who told you that?"

"Oh, you know, small-town gossip."

She narrows her eyes at me like she's trying to think of who she might have told. And did they snitch about it to me. "Yes, I have been hoping to expand my business for a while. This space would be perfect because I wouldn't have to move."

"But if it would be so beneficial for you to expand, why not go elsewhere, to begin with?" I ask. I notice the lawyer is no longer scribbling on his notepad. He hasn't looked up at us, but I'm sure he's listening in.

"As I'm sure you know, land is at a premium here in Crested Peaks. I haven't been able to find another location that would be suitable for my needs. This, however, is perfect because my contractors could simply remove the wall between the two places."

"Did you want it badly enough to kill over, though?"

Okay, so maybe I went over the line on that one.

"Excuse me?" she huffs. "You seriously think I'd kill over a little real estate?"

"If it meant you could do three times the business you're doing now, then maybe?"

"Seriously, who told you all of this?"

By now, her face is bright pink, and her fists are balled up at her sides. I hope she doesn't take a swing at me, but this is crucial. I'm fighting to save this town and my business, and if I have to take a punch to do it, then so be it.

"I swear, I only heard it through the grapevine." Sure, it's the alley cat grapevine, but whatever. It's still a grapevine, right?

"How dare you!" she shouts as she stomps out the door.

Yikes. I glance over at the lawyer, who hasn't even looked up at us.

I turn and hurry out the door, hoping I don't get jumped by Abby on the way back to Marcall's.

Chapter Twelve

When I get back to the cafe, I show Damien the lawyer's business card and fill him in on what happened.

"You seriously told her what the animals told you?" Damien asks.

"Sure! I wanted to see how she'd react."

"And?"

"She's furious. I thought for a moment she was going to take a swing at me; she was so angry. She had her fists all squeezed up at her sides."

"I suppose getting punched is better than getting held at gunpoint, like usual. But geez, boss, you need to be careful."

"Anyway, I don't think we're any closer to where we were before I went over there."

"Do you think Abby would kill Jack over real estate?"

"It's worth a lot of money. Plus, she was agitated over the fact that she insists that all those sketchy people kept visiting the toy store."

"She could make that up, don't you think?"

"She filed a bunch of complaints with the county. I don't get the sense that she's lying about that though."

"But it still doesn't explain what those people were doing at the toy store in the middle of the night," Damien points out. He holds up one finger. "We have a questionable motive. But let's say for now that her wanting that valuable space is a reason to kill."

"Go on."

He holds up a second finger. "She claims she was baking the night of the party, but she hasn't offered any corroboration."

"Right."

He holds up a third finger. "What's her means, though? I'm assuming you don't just walk into your local drugstore and pick up a box of roofys, right?"

"That's a good question. Where *do* you get those things?" I ask.

"I think they're illegal, aren't they?"

"That would be something we should ask Drew," I add.

Then, as if on cue, Drew walks into Marcall's. "Hey guys," he says. "I came to check out the watch you found."

"Stumpy found it," Damien informs him.

"Uh oh, I suppose that means it was in his mouth?"

"He dug it out of a pile of snow across the street, brought it in here, and then handed it to me. So not only does it have cat slobber on it, but I'm also afraid I handled it. I had no idea it was evidence at first. I'm so sorry."

Drew slides on a pair of latex gloves. "That's okay, let me see it," he wiggles his fingers to say hand it over.

Damien holds out a plastic bag that he must have put the watch in while I was gone. Drew takes it out and examines it carefully. "Where exactly did he find this?"

"It was across the street, in that snow pile right there." I point out the window.

"So, we don't even know if this is part of the crime scene or if someone accidentally dropped it."

"But the crystal face is broken, and the clasp is bent like it was ripped off someone's wrist. I think it was damaged in the struggle between the killer and Will."

Drew gives me one of those looks that says he's tolerating what he often thinks are my far-fetched stories.

"Didn't you say it ended up in the pile of snow because of the sidewalk plow?"

"Oh. Uh, yeah."

"So, it could have been dropped on the sidewalk by accident and then damaged when the sidewalk plow came through? Those things are pretty powerful."

"I suppose. But it looks a lot like a watch I saw in the sketches that Will was trying to hide from me." I point out.

"When we searched the toy store after Will disappeared, I didn't find any sketches, by the way."

Rats. Why do I seem to run into a roadblock at every turn?

"I'll take this back to the station, though, and have it dusted for fingerprints and check it out. But don't get your hopes up because I'm still not convinced this is part of Will's attack."

"Okay, I understand."

Before Drew can say anything further, Abby bursts into the cafe, and if I thought she was mad before, she was clearly just getting started because now she's outraged.

"You called the Tribune on me?" she bellows, waving her phone in the air.

"What? No! I didn't call anybody! What are you talking about?" I'm afraid to get too close to her for fear she really will attack me this time.

She thrusts her phone in my face so I can read the article while Drew, completely taken aback by all of this, appears ready to take action if need be. Damien darts from the kitchen like he, too, is ready to defend me. Meanwhile, he and I both stare open-mouthed at the headline on the Crested Peaks Tribune website.

Crested Peaks Store Owner Willing to Kill for Land?

I stand there slack-jawed, reading the hit piece someone put together regarding Abby's plans to expand into the toy store. I hold my hands up to show my confusion about all of this.

"I swear to you I haven't mentioned this to any reporter. If someone else knows about this, it must be from you."

"You confronted me about this in the toy store, so you obviously knew! Someone else knows, and you're going to tell me who it is right now!" she growls, taking a step toward me.

Drew lunges forward, putting an arm between us while Damien jumps in front of me.

"All right, ladies, simmer down," Drew orders.

"Ms. Hooper, why don't you take a seat here. Charlotte, you sit down over there. Let's all take a breath and talk about this like the calm, rational adults I know you are."

Damien grabs a seat and pushes me into it while Drew does the same with Abby. Talk about looking like a killer! This woman is out of control!

"She was in the toy shop today confronting me about wanting to expand my bakery. I only told one other person that, and he swears he never repeated that. I want to know how she knows about it."

Drew turns to me, placing his hands on his hips and glaring at me. "You were in the toy shop again today?"

Drat. Abby has a big mouth.

"I stopped by after you went to the hospital with Will. I thought someone might be around, and I wanted to ask them if they had any more information." I know that sounds lame. But it's the most I will say in front of Abby.

"Frost's lawyer was in there, and I wanted to see what he knew, too. I walk in there, and she," she stabs a bony finger in my direction, "confronted me with questions about my wanting to expand my business."

"May I ask how you came about this information?" Drew looks at me again.

I respond with a look that he knows by now means I got it from the animals. But if I admit that out loud, the whole town will think I've lost it for sure this time.

Everyone knows I'm a witch, but only a handful of people know about the talking rabbits. It's common for witches and wizards to have familiars with whom they share a special bond. But actual talking familiars are uncommon.

The last thing I need is for the general public to know about my enchanted animal friends. It's even more important to keep it safe, especially now that we know Poppy can communicate with all three of them.

Drew sighs and shakes his head. "Never mind that for now. I have a question for you, Ms. Hooper."

She looks up at him, surprised that he's now focused on questioning her.

"Can you tell me where you were when Jack Frost was killed? When he drank the spiked peppermint martini?"

"Like I already told her." She sneers at me, "I was in the bakery working. It's a very busy time of year for me, and I was working late at night on Christmas orders."

"Can anyone corroborate that statement?" Drew asks.

She looks deflated and shakes her head.

"You made a brief trip to Mexico last month, yes?" he asks.

Now we all look surprised. How did he know she went to Mexico, and what does that matter?

"I did. Why are you asking?"

"Our records show you were only there for two days. That's an awfully brief trip for someone flying in from Colorado," he points out.

"I had to come back early for work. Do I need a lawyer here or something?"

"You tell me," Drew says.

I have to bite my tongue to keep from going *ohhhhhhh*. Drew means business when he talks like that. I should know. I've been on the receiving end of that question.

"I don't have to take any of this!" she announces jumping up from her seat and stomping toward the door. "You watch your step!" she exclaims, throwing the door open and marching out into the cold.

"What was that bit about Mexico? I don't understand why that's important."

"Roofys are illegal in the United States." Drew starts.

"Told you," Damien says, smacking me on the arm.

I stare at Drew in shock. "You think she went to Mexico to get drugs to poison Jack?"

"I don't know, but that's why I asked her. It's a possibility."

"Any word on Will's condition?" Damien asks.

"Nope. He's in a coma. The hospital is under strict orders to call me the second he wakes up. *If* he wakes up," he adds.

"He could hold the key to everything!" I exclaim. "He has to wake up."

Chapter Thirteen

The following morning, once again, I'm relieved to see Gladys walk in the door at 6:30 like always. It may seem silly but having that one constant every morning always makes me feel better. Not that she'd ever miss, but still, as quiet as things have been, I'm starting to worry.

"So, what's new with the case?" she asks.

"I was hoping you had fresh information." I tell her.

"Fresh information has been difficult to come by with everyone staying home I'm afraid."

"How about I tell you what I know, and you can fill in the details if you have any."

"Go for it!" Gladys exclaims.

"I think one of the suspects is Scarlett Wise. But she claims she left the party early, because she had a migraine, and took a ride share and therefore has proof of leaving the party."

"I know why she left the party early, and it wasn't a migraine." Gladys responds.

"It wasn't?"

Gladys snorts. "Heck no! Jack Frost had a restraining order against her."

"He what? She didn't tell me that!"

"She tried to run him over with her car once, and he took out a restraining order against her."

"I assume this all stems from the lawsuit?" I ask.

"It does! I heard she tried to approach him at the party, but her brother grabbed her and pulled her away from him. Put her in a cab and sent her home."

"But if she went home early, then how could she have spiked his drink?" I muse.

"Her brother could have done it easily."

"How's that?" I ask.

"He's a bartender at the Hotel Glacier. He was working the night of the party."

My mouth forms an O as I stare at Gladys wide eyed. "Gladys, have I ever told you that you're our best customer of all time? Breakfast is on me today!"

Gladys laughs. "I didn't tell you anything that everyone else didn't already know."

"But *I* didn't know that. And I didn't know how Scarlett could have spiked Frost's drink if she left early. I had motive for her, and now I know she had an opportunity to spike the drink. You may have blown the case wide open Gladys!"

"I'm happy to be of assistance dear. We have to do something to save this town."

"I'll get Drew over here as soon as I can to tell him the latest."

"And if I hear anything particularly juicy, I'll let you know!" she tells me.

The moment Gladys leaves I call Drew and ask him to stop by when he can.

"You haven't been at the toy store again, have you?" he sighs.

"I haven't," I assure him. "But I have some new information I think you should hear about."

"Okay. I'm running down a lead myself, but I'll stop by when I get a chance."

When Drew finally stops in several hours later he's grim faced.

"Oh great, what now?" I moan.

"It's not exactly bad news, but I'm not sure how you'll take it."

"Lay it on me!" I tell him.

"Abby showed up at the police station today with a delivery driver in tow," Drew tells us.

"A delivery driver?" I ask. "Why would she do that?"

"He corroborated her alibi for the night Jack was killed."

"No way! That seems way too convenient," I argue.

"He had a huge delivery of sugar and flour for her but had a flat tire on the way up from Denver and was delayed trying to get it replaced. So, he couldn't get there until late at night, and she just happened to be there working."

"I don't believe that for a second! Why didn't she say something before? Why did she sit right here and tell you there was no one to corroborate her story?"

"She told it was late at night, and she was tired and completely forgot that he had shown up. She also told me she was so busy she let him in the back door, and he unloaded the supplies and left. They barely talked, so she forgot he was there."

"Please tell me you don't believe this!" I beg.

"I talked to the guy myself, *and* I called his supervisor. He's been on the job for 17 years, never had so much as a parking ticket. He completely checks out, as does his GPS system that's outfitted on all their delivery vehicles. The records show he was there exactly when Abby claims he was."

"Now it's looking more than ever like Scarlett is our killer. Did you know Jack took out a restraining order against her?"

"I know that, but how did you know that?"

"Gladys told me."

"Naturally."

"Are you going to arrest her?"

"On what grounds?"

"She's threatened him publicly! She's threatened him in writing! She tried to run him over with her car!"

"Charlotte, you need to calm down. I know all of these things, and the CPPD is investigating this thoroughly. You have to know that."

"I do," I hang my head. "You know her brother is a bartender at the Hotel Glacier. He could have slipped the roofie into Jack's drink even though Scarlett had already gone home."

"We are questioning everyone who's even remotely related to this case. You just have to give us time to work the case."

"I don't know how you can stand to be so patient throughout. It drives me crazy!" I announce bobbing up and down on my toes I'm so agitated.

"Gosh, I never noticed," Drew laughs.

Chapter Fourteen

"Anybody home?" Damien calls out as he, Tom, Bubbles, and Poppy come into the cafe. I told him to take the day off to show Poppy around town, visit with the new Santa, and enjoy some hot chocolate and cookies.

"Hey there! How was your day?"

"It was great!" Poppy exclaims. "Where are my boys?"

She now refers to Marshall, Marcus, and Stumpy as her boys. She loves to visit with them and dress them up in costumes. They don't love being dressed up and paraded around like they're live dolls, but they tolerate her. I'm not sure they have a choice. She's quite stubborn.

"They're in the back," I tell her. "They might be napping, but if you give the rabbits a blueberry, I'm sure they'll be happy to see you." Let's face it. Perhaps the only reason they tolerate her so well is she's always offering them treats—their favorite pastime.

"Hold this, please," she says, handing me the stuffed unicorn I got for her last month at Santa's Workshop. I stare down at it, thinking about how much has changed since I bought it a few short weeks ago. The toy store won't even be there much longer.

"Wow," Tom marvels. "I can't believe she let you hold that thing. She carries it everywhere and won't let anyone else touch it."

"Maybe because I'm the one who gave it to her?" I offer.

Moments later, Poppy reappears, dropping blueberries on the floor while Marcus and Marshall follow behind her, gobbling up as many as they can chew.

She points at the unicorn stuffie. "Is she alive too?"

I look down at the toy. "No, not like Marshall and Marcus, anyway. She's for fun and your imagination."

"But she has a heartbeat."

I look at Tom and Damien. "Can she get any sweeter? She thinks she has a heartbeat."

"She does," Poppy insists.

"You mean you pretend she has a heartbeat?" I ask. I'm completely confused about what to say at this point. I don't have any kids yet, so I'm not always sure how to talk to Poppy.

Poppy looks at me like the rabbits do when they think I'm too dense for words. She marches over to me, takes it from me, and presses it up against her ear. "She has a heartbeat."

Then she hands her toy back to me. I press my head against the unicorn and nearly drop it when I hear the distinct sound of a watch ticking from inside. I stare at Tom and Damien, my eyes huge with shock.

"What is it? Are you messing with us?" Damien asks.

I jab my head toward Poppy in such a way that Tom realizes I need to tell Damien something alone.

"Hey princess, let's see if we can find a treat for Stumpy in the fridge, okay?" he says, leading her back toward the kitchen.

"There's some cheese in the fridge," Damien tells them. "Try that."

After Poppy is safely out of earshot, Damien leans in. "What is wrong with you?"

I press the unicorn against his ear. "Whoa. Is that a watch ticking?"

"Either that or a tiny bomb! I have to get the watch out," I hiss at Damien.

"If you ruin that unicorn, Poppy will hex you," he hisses back.

"She doesn't know how to hex!" I insist.

"Have you ever seen a three-year-old throw a tantrum?" he asks, raising one eyebrow at me.

I glance back toward the kitchen, hoping Tom is still keeping her entertained back there.

"Hey honey, why don't you guys make us all some hot chocolate while you're back there?"

Tom sticks his head through the serving window. "You want *me* to make hot chocolate? I don't know where anything is."

Damien points at the unicorn.

"Ohhhh, okayyyyy. Poppy, it looks like we're making hot chocolate."

"Yayyyyy!" Poppy shouts.

I concentrate on the seam running down the middle of the unicorn's stomach, opening it stitch by stitch; when I finally get a wide enough opening, I stick my fingers inside, feeling around the cottony fluff. When my fingers brush against the cold, hard watch, I pull it out.

"Whoa," Damien whispers.

I don't have to know watches to know this is rare and expensive.

"You hold it," I thrust it toward Damien.

"Why do I have to hold it? You're going to get me in trouble!"

"Because I have to put the unicorn parts back!"

Damien shakes his head, but then pulls a handkerchief from his pocket and takes the watch with it. He wraps it up carefully and places it on the table.

As I start to stitch the unicorn back together magically, he grabs my hand. "Wait! She'll wonder where its heartbeat went."

"You honestly think she'll notice?" I ask.

"She'll think you killed it!"

"You two sound like a couple of leaky balloons in there with all the whispering," Tom calls out.

"We're almost done! How's the hot chocolate going?" Damien asks.

"We're waiting for the water to boil."

"Can't you give it a magic heartbeat?" he asks.

"Oh yeah, good idea." I glance around the room for something I can enchant when I think to pull a quarter from my pocket. "I hope this works," I mutter as I focus on making it sound like a heartbeat.

I quickly stuff it into the unicorn and sew it back up. The stitches aren't as perfect as they were before, but they will have to do. I scoop up the watch and head back to the kitchen, where I lock it in the file cabinet in my office.

"You guys need some help in here?" I ask handing the unicorn back to Poppy, who immediately presses it to her ear and smiles. Phew. Good thing Damien remembered the heartbeat, because I certainly wouldn't have. Children are complicated.

We all enjoy our hot chocolate with peppermint sticks and marshmallows, but I'm distracted by the discovery of the watch. First Will was hiding sketches of them. Then we find one near where he was attacked. And now there's one inside of a toy which I have to assume was hidden there on purpose. What the heck is going on here?

"You'll call Drew about the watch as soon as we're done here, right?" Damien demands.

"I promise I'll call him!" And I mean it.

"Hey, I was just going to call you," he says the moment he picks up the phone.

"To tell me what a fabulous girlfriend I am?" I laugh.

"Yes, and to tell you, we discovered that the watch that Stumpy found on the sidewalk is an Omega Seamaster."

"That sounds like a very expensive watch."

"Expensive and stolen. The serial number confirmed it."

"I'm not sure what any of this means, but I have news for you as well." I fill him in on the watch we found in Poppy's unicorn.

"I'll be right over," he says, hanging up abruptly once again. When Drew is on a case, he has tunnel vision, and I've learned it's useless to convince him otherwise.

He's the youngest detective in the CPPD history, and I think he feels like he needs to prove himself on every case. Unfortunately, that means I don't get to see him as often as I'd like, but I understand his drive to prove himself.

I feel the same way about this cafe. My grandma loved this place and this town, and I refuse to go down without a fight. We'll find Santa's killer, and we'll get back to normal around here if I have anything to say about it.

As I patiently wait for Drew to arrive, he texts me.

Will Flemming is awake. On my way to hospital now. Stay put!

Rats! I really, really want to go to the hospital and be there when Drew questions Will, but I'm also trying hard not to run off on my own every chance I get.

It's not just my safety I have to think about now. Both Damien and Aranya were nearly killed last month because of me, and it isn't right that I endanger them for my own gain. It's torture waiting for Drew, and I check my phone every five seconds, hoping to hear something.

Finally, after what seems like days, my phone pings with a text from Drew.

Jack Frost was smuggling black market luxury watches through the toy store. Will found out and was blackmailing him. He was coming to talk to you and ask for help when he was attacked. He doesn't know who

bashed him over the head. Be careful and don't go any-where! I'll be right there.

I'm about to text him back when Scarlett walks in the door. I'm so startled I nearly drop the phone. My heart races when I think about how she may be here to kill me.

Does she know that Will's awake? But then I wonder what her lawsuit has to do with stolen priceless watches. And what if her killing Frost had nothing to do with the watches? This is all swirling around in my head as I stare at her, dumbfounded.

"Hey, I have something I need to tell you." She tilts her head at me, no doubt wondering why I'm staring at her like a deer in the headlights. "Is something wrong?" she asks.

"How did you know?" I ask.

"Oh please. It took about ten seconds to figure out you weren't reporters. And your donuts are famous in case you didn't know."

"But you let us into your house." I stammer. I'm so embarrassed. And still a little worried she might try something.

"You had free donuts. Why wouldn't I let you in?" She laughs. "But I'm not here about that. My lawyers told me something that I thought you might like to know. Since you seem to be investigating Frost's murder and all."

"Yeah, sure, have a seat," I tell her, pointing to the nearest chair. I'm hoping if I can keep her talking long enough, Drew will get here. In case she decides to take another victim. As long as I can keep her talking, maybe I can ask her about the watches.

"Oh, this won't take long. I wanted you to know that I had my lawyers reach out to Frost's lawyer to let him know we're still suing the estate. I'm going to prove that the toy was my idea in the first place and that he stole it. Now that he's dead, I should be able to get the patent on it, and the toy companies will have to deal directly with me and my attorneys instead."

"Oh. Okay. Why are you telling me this, though?" This has been a wild day, and maybe my brain is a little fuzzy, but I'm still confused.

"Because, when my attorneys tried to find him, they couldn't."

"He left town?"

She sighs in exasperation. "No, dummy, he doesn't exist."

"But I met him. I talked to him in person. He gave me his card!" I insist.

"He's not a lawyer! He doesn't work for the firm that's printed on his card. There's no law license. Nothing! He's a ghost. Hey, are you okay? You look you've *seen* a ghost."

Chapter Fifteen

The rest of the afternoon was a whirlwind of activity. Drew collected the watch from me and then talked to Scarlett's lawyers. Once they realized that Leo Price must have been in cahoots with Jack and his watch smuggling operation they went into high gear.

I swore to be on my best behavior and not interfere with any of it. I decide to hang out at Bean Around a Bit instead and taste test some new coffee that Miranda ordered. We're sipping espresso and discussing what could happen next when Marshall, Marcus, and Stumpy barrel into the shop while a customer opens the door for them.

"Lady!" they shout.

"What now?" I groan.

"They took them!"

"Who's they? And who's them? What are you talking about? Calm down and talk slower."

"Some bad people came with guns and wanted to know where the watch was. When Damien and Aranya said they didn't know, the bad guys made them leave, and they left a note for you.

"When we heard them shouting, we hid behind the door. Is that okay? Stumpy thought we should try biting them on the ankles like we did that mean lady last time, but there were too many of them, and they looked extra mean. Not just crazy like the other lady."

Before they can even finish their story, I bolt from the coffee shop running to the cafe as fast as I can. I throw open the front door as I scream out Damien and Aranya's names. The cafe is eerily silent, and there are several chairs and tables knocked on their side. It looks like they put up a fight. I see a crumpled note on the counter and snatch it up with shaky hands.

I have your people. Meet me with the watch at 2 PM in the town square and come alone. If you call the cops, your friends are dead.

By now, Miranda is peering over my shoulder, reading the note.

"Please tell me you aren't seriously considering not calling the cops," she begs.

"Of course, I'm calling the cops."

If anything happens to Damien and Aranya, I'll never forgive myself.

I call Drew but I can barely explain what happened I'm so distraught. When he finally understands what I'm trying to tell him it seems like he and half the CPPD are at Marcall's within seconds.

There are officers swarming the café talking on phones and tapping on computers. Miranda keeps everyone stocked with coffee as the force discusses options for getting Damien and Aranya back while catching the crooks at the same time.

"Thanks to your description of this 'Leo Price' character we were able to track him back to a gang that's been on the most wanted list," Drew's captain tells me.

"A gang?" I ask.

"A highly organized, well-disciplined gang of jewelry thieves who have apparently been funneling stolen watches through the toy store for years," he explains.

"And right under our noses the entire time," I marvel.

"Yep." He nods. "It was the perfect front. Watches are small and easy to smuggle. And as you discovered," he points at me, "easy to hide within a child's toy if necessary."

"That's all dandy and I'll leave that up to you to sort out, but I need to know how to get my friends back," I plead. "I'll do whatever is necessary. Just give me the watch back and I'll take it to the town square at 2:00."

"Charlotte, you won't be the one to drop off the watch. You're not law enforcement and it's too dangerous. I won't allow it," Drew lectures me.

"The note says that *I* have to come alone."

"I don't care what it says. We're using a decoy. We have a female officer who has a similar build. We'll put a wig on her and catch Price when we make the exchange."

"And then what? When he realizes it isn't me, he'll refuse to tell us where he has Damien and Aranya."

"We'll get it out of him once we grab him," Drew assures me.

As Drew and I continue to argue, I get a text from Price with a picture of Damien and Aranya in a room, but I can't tell where it is.

They have exactly 3.5 hours of oxygen left. As soon as I have the watch and I'm safely on my way out of town, I'll tell you where the underground bunker is.

"Drew, this is serious. If he gets the watch, and your officer attempts to grab him, he won't tell us where the bunker is. I have to make the drop, and we have to let him go."

"You know we can't just let him go, Char."

"She has a point," Drew's captain says. "What if we let her make the drop off--"

"--no way," Drew cuts him off.

"Let me finish," the captain says. "We place a tracker on the watch; Ms. Duffin here makes the drop while we're all watching. Price gets the watch and tells us where the victims are being held. Once the victims are safe, we trace the watch to him and grab him up."

"Remember, I can use witchcraft if Price tries anything funny at the exchange." I plead with Drew. I've never been so sure of anything in my life. I don't even care about the town at this point. I need to save my friends.

"All right," Drew shakes his head and sighs. "I don't like it one bit, but I also know there's now talking either one of you out of this."

His captain and I nod grimly at each other.

"You have to understand, this is my fault, Drew. I continuously put myself and my friends in danger, and now there's a huge price to pay. I'm a horrible friend. I'm no better than my parents."

"Stop that!" Drew snaps at me. "You've actually done everything right this time."

I look at him in surprise.

"Well, almost everything," he smiles. "I obviously don't approve of you questioning suspects and searching for clues, but this time, you did the right thing by contacting me right away when it was crucial.

"And you had no idea that Poppy's unicorn was hiding a Patek Philippe watch. And now you're willing to risk your safety to rescue your friends. You are nothing like your parents, and I don't ever want to hear that come out of your mouth again. Your grandma would be proud."

I'm not sure whether I should cry or hug him or both, but it doesn't matter because the captain approaches us again with instructions about how the drop-off will proceed.

I'll meet with Price at the town square to hand over the watch. I'll be wearing a wire, so when he tells me where to find the bunker, several officers will be on standby to race to the location, saving Damien and Aranya.

Meanwhile, once I'm safely away from him, the rest of the force will move in on him via the tracker and snatch him up.

What could go wrong?

As one technician carefully wires me up, another works on placing a tiny tracking chip inside the back of the watch. "I get that it's obviously a luxury watch and all, but how much could that be worth, that Price would risk everything to get it back?" I ask them.

The technician working on the watch snickers. "How much do you think this is actually worth?"

"I don't know," I respond, glancing back and forth between them. "A few thousand?"

I'm a little insulted when they both laugh this time.

"Try $2 million, honey," the woman wiring me up tells me.

Gulp. "You're kidding me, right?"

When they both shake their heads, I have to sit down I feel so lightheaded. "You're telling me that I bought a stuffed animal that had a $2 million watch hidden inside, and none of us knew the difference?"

"That particular toy clearly wasn't supposed to be sold. It must have been an accident, and when they realized you're the one they sold it to, they went after you," the technician points out.

Hearing this makes me want to vomit. If they had figured this out earlier and realized Poppy had the unicorn... I can't finish the thought in my own head. And the idea that Frost was using the toy store in Crested Peaks to do this. Now I'm beyond angry.

Poppy could have been hurt. Damien and Aranya are who knows where, probably scared out of their minds, wondering if they'll ever see their loved ones again. And to top it all off, the crooks have nearly ruined this town. There is no way

Price is getting away with this. Even if I have to chase him down myself.

After a lengthy lecture from Drew about how I'm not to try anything foolish, even though I'm so mad I could spit nails, the CPPD sends me off to the town square. I have the watch in my purse, and the wired microphone is taped discreetly to my skin underneath my shirt.

My heart is pounding so hard I'm surprised people in the park can't hear it. Then I'm afraid that the nervous sweat running down my back will short out the wire, and I'll shock myself. "Can you guys hear my heartbeat?" I whisper.

"Stop talking to yourself," Drew scolds me in my earpiece. "You'll look suspicious."

"Yes, sir," I grumble. It's so weird. People are milling about, all around me, minding their own business, going about their day without a care in the world. In the middle of it all I'm trying to catch an infamous jewel thief and save my friends lives. I really need to stop getting mixed up in these kinds of things.

And If I thought my pulse was racing before, it thumps double time when I spot Price up ahead. There are undercover cops spread throughout the park, all keeping a careful eye on me, but this is still terrifying. There's about a thousand things that could go wrong here, and my friends' lives are at stake. And I really want to throw up right now.

Price approaches me, planting himself directly in front of me.

"You have the watch?"

"Yes," I stammer.

"Then hand it over, you idiot."

"There's no need for name calling, you know."

He rolls his eyes at me. "Just give me the watch."

"Where are my friends?" I demand.

"Hand me the watch. Then I tell you where I'm keeping your friends."

"Fine," I mutter while I try to unzip my purse. My hands are shaking so badly I can barely get the zipper open. I finally hold out the watch, and he snatches it from my grasp.

"Where are my friends?" I beg while I grab his arm, squeezing as hard as I can, hoping to appeal to whatever tiny shred of humanity he may have left.

"Hold your horses, lady. I have to check one thing," he growls at me, jerking his arm back.

Uh oh. When he pulls a plastic mechanism out of his pocket, I try to snatch the watch back, but he's too quick. I see several of the police officers, who are planted in strategic locations, freeze. This can't be good.

He waves the small bar over the watch, and when it emits several high-pitched beeps, I know I'm in serious trouble. "You fool, you just killed your friends," he says throwing the watch at my feet. Then he spins on his heel, and takes off through the crowded square, zig zagging through shoppers and jumping over bushes to get away.

"Stop!" I shout, but as I start to chase after him myself, one of the CPPD officers grabs me, refusing to let go.

Drew rushes up to us. "Drew! Tell him to let me go! I have to go after him! I have to find out where Damien and Aranya are! They could die!"

"Charlotte, it's too dangerous for you to chase him. Let the police do what they're trained to do."

"But we have to find out where Damien and Aranya are!" I plead with him. "Where are the underground bunkers in Crested Peaks? I've never even heard of them!"

"We have every available person working on it," the officer who's still holding on to me explains. "They must be old because no one else seems to have heard of them either, but we're doing everything we can. We're guessing they date back to at least the 1960s, but we're not sure."

Drew and I turn to each other. "Harvey!" we chorus.

Chapter Sixteen

"I'll take care of her now!" Drew tells the officer as he releases me, and we run for his car. Drew flies down Main Street, lights and sirens screaming. If the circumstances weren't so dire, I'd realize how fun this is.

For once, it's not me on the waiting end of the sirens. Now I'm the sirens. I wonder if I can talk Drew into doing this again sometime when someone's life isn't at stake. I'm guessing the answer will be no.

We pull up in front of the Hotel Glacier and park in the fire zone. No wonder Drew loves being a cop. He gets to break all the rules. We jump out of the car and scramble up the steps, calling out, "Harvey! Harvey! It's an emergency!"

And just like that, Harvey pops out of nowhere in front of us.

"Goodness, gracious, what is happening? You scared me half to death. I was in the west end of the hotel lecturing a maid on the proper storage of a fitted bed sheet. Why is it that no one knows how to--"

"Harvey!" I shout, interrupting his speech.

"Yes, miss?"

"This is literally a matter of life and death. Damien and Aranya are trapped in an underground bunker in Crested Peaks. Do you know where any of them are?" I ask, on the verge of tears. I'm so scared he'll say no.

"Why, of course, I know where they are. They're a bit outside of town on Route 4, past Peanut Lake. There's a bright red arrow sign on the first right. At least that's what I'm told," he adds.

"It's our best shot. Thank you, Harvey! If you were alive, I'd kiss you!"

"Aw shucks," he murmurs, looking at the ground, and if I didn't know any better, I'd say he blushed. Can ghosts blush?

Drew and I jump back in his car and speed off toward Route 4.

"How long will it take us to get there?"

"It's about ten minutes away if we're lucky," Drew says grimly.

"We don't have a second to lose!" I announce, grabbing his arm to steady myself as he careens around a corner.

"Oh! And one more thing!" I announce.

"You're telling me 'one more thing' at a time like this?"

"When I grabbed your arm, it made me think of it."

"Well, spit it out!" he demands.

"If your officers don't catch Price, I can."

"Char, what did you do?"

"When I grabbed his arm, I secretly placed an enchanted tracer on his shirt."

"You used magic to tag the jewelry thief?" Drew asks, sounding more impressed than I've ever heard him sound.

"I did."

"Cool," he nods his head and grins at me. "That's some good police work."

"You think?"

"You're still not an actual police officer though," he wags his finger at me.

"You may not believe this, but after today I don't want to be!"

He definitely doesn't believe me.

"Can you go any faster?" I plead. "We have to make it on time."

As Drew flies up the hill, I pray we'll make it. Poppy can't lose her foster dad, and Aranya's family will be devastated if something happens to their daughter. And I can't bear to lose my friends. We must save them.

"Breathe, Char, breathe," Drew reminds me.

Oh yeah, good idea. I'm not sure how long I've been holding my breath.

"There! Right there is the arrow Harvey told us about!"

Drew swings a sharp right as the back end of his car skids back and forth. It's a good thing he knows how to drive like this, because I certainly don't. I glance back when I hear sirens behind us.

We called for an ambulance and backup on the way up here, and they're starting to catch up. I count them all after the turn. One, two, three, four - wow, this is a lot of backup - five, six. Two ambulances and four additional police cars follow us.

"There! Off to the left!" I shout, waving my hand wildly in Drew's face.

He skids to a stop as we leap from the car. The sun is setting and the flashing lights from all the vehicles bounce off the sides of the mountain and reflect on the snow. It's all so eerie looking.

We would never have found this without Harvey's help. A small sign reads "Warning: No Trespassing" next to a set of stairs. There are fresh tire tracks and footprints all around us, so I'm sure we're in the right place.

Drew runs down the stairs first and curses when he sees the huge padlock and chain around the door. It takes a mere second of concentration, and I do it while running for me to pop open the lock.

Drew turns to me, his face beaming. "Way to go!"

He throws the padlock to the ground, pulling on the huge chain that's intertwined through the door handle, throwing it on the ground as well. He jerks open the heavy steel door, and Damien and Aranya rush at us, nearly knocking both of us over.

"Oh, thank goodness!" Aranya cries as she hangs on to me for dear life.

"Thanks, man," Damien tells Drew as they throw their arms around each other. "I was getting a little nervous there."

"Are you guys okay?" Drew asks.

"I think we're pretty good," Damien tells us. "A few bruises here and there and a scratch or two, but otherwise, we're okay, right, Aranya?"

Aranya nods tearfully, still unable to talk. I help her up the stairs into the waiting hands of the paramedics while Drew and Damien follow behind us.

"We'll meet you at the hospital," Drew explains while the officers who followed us gather for an update.

"Status on Price?" Drew asks.

"We got him Detective!"

"Yes!" I shout throwing my fist in the air.

"We lost him for a short time, but your friend Miranda," the officer nods at me, "told us she was sure you'd put an enchantment on him if you got the chance, and I guess you did because she helped us track him down then," he says scratching his head. "Craziest thing I ever saw."

"Way to go honey!" Drew says giving me a big hug.

"I'm so glad it actually worked!" I exclaim.

Chapter Seventeen

O nce again, we're nearly kicked out of the Emergency Room at the hospital for celebrating too loudly. I'm surprised the staff lets us in here at all. We seem to come here a lot. And we always break the rules.

"We have a surprise and some wonderful news for all of you," Tom announces as he and Damien grin at each other. "They finally located a cousin of Poppy's in Puerto Rico."

The rest of us fall silent. I'm happy for Poppy if they've found her family, but that also means she'll be sent back to Puerto Rico to live with this cousin. I'm not sure why Tom and Damien think this is good news. I know they were hoping to adopt her permanently, and we've all come to love her.

"Oh," I say, while trying to plaster a fake smile on my face.

"That's not the best part," Damien says. "But the look on your faces is priceless."

"Are you messing with us?" Drew asks.

"Just a little," he pauses and grins again. "The cousin wasn't even aware that his cousin, Poppy's mom, had a daughter. And when he learned she had been living in a loving foster home, that wants to adopt her permanently, he happily agreed to sign over any rights to her. As soon as the county gets the paperwork, they'll begin the permanent adoption process immediately."

We cheer so loudly I'm convinced the night nurse is going to beat us all with an IV pole. "It's my last warning!" she scolds, wagging a finger at us.

"Oh! And I almost forgot! Rita stopped by with some good news when you were over at Miranda's, boss." Damien tells me.

"You mean before you were kidnapped?"

"Yes!"

Rita is the woman who owns Marcall's building, in addition to the building next door. After two unfortunate, and even disastrous tenants, she has taken a long time searching for a new one.

"Uh oh, please tell me she isn't selling the place."

"No, not at all! She found a new tenant for next door!"

"That's great! Who is it?"

"It's a candy store!"

We all look at each other and smile. A candy store could be fun. And safe, I hope. Assuming it isn't owned by mobsters or anything.

"They aren't selling peppermint candy, are they?" I ask while everyone groans at my dumb joke. "What? Too soon?" I shrug.

Thank you for reading Peppermints & Pandemonium!
Sign up for my email list here:
https://mailchi.mp/9ebce0da866a/email-signup-list
Visit my website

biskinnerauthor.com
Follow me on Instagram @bethiskinner Facebook @biskinnerauthor TikTok @biskinner